MW01519049

OVERWHELM

SIMON SHADOWS

ANTIENTROPIC PRESS

Editing by Kaija Rayne.

Published by Antientropic Press.
www.antrientropic.press

First Edition / April 2023

This is a work of fiction. Names, characters, business, events and incidents are the products of the author's imagination. Any resemblance to actual persons, living or dead, or actual events is purely coincidental.

ISBN 979-8-9878446-3-2

10 9 8 7 6 5 4 3 2

CONTENT WARNINGS

The stories in this anthology explore a variety of sensitive subjects. Please read with care.

KILLER

Abuse

Blood and gore

Mental illness

Murder

Self-harm

Substance use and addiction

ANOMALOUS

Abuse

Blood and gore

Homophobia

Mentions of child abuse (no scenes)

Religious trauma

Sexual imagery

Violence

DUE SOUTH

Blood and gore

Substance use and addiction

Violence

SYMMETRY

Blood and gore

CONJUGATION

Blood

Classism

Substance use and addiction

OVERWHELM

For Gus, Liv, and Alex.

*Thank you for helping me get through
my own year of overwhelm.*

CONTENTS

INTRODUCTION

I have always loved horror, but I'm picky about what actually scares me.

Don't get me wrong; I love mainstays of the genre like werewolves and ghosts and demonic possession, but they've always felt more like fantasy to me than anything particularly frightening. I grew up on the early 00's Internet, soaking in the deep weirdness of creepypasta like Slenderman, the Russian Sleep Experiments, and SCPs, stories of humans interacting with forces outside of anything they've experienced in life or in movie tropes, and those were the kind of stories that stuck with me. The idea of being stalked by a vampire might be thrilling in a sort of fear-for-one's-body sense, but to evoke that chilling, pit-of-the-stomach sense of terror that makes me keep the lights on at night, I crave stories about things I've never seen before, things whose motives I cannot begin to predict.

Additionally, science has always been a source of inspiration, wonder, and horror for me. I'm fascinated by the contradiction between how huge my existence seems to me and the simultaneous, objective knowledge that I am a meaningless and temporary pattern of organic chemical processes. There is little I find more terrifying than the prospect of an encounter with something that reminds me of my essential tininess, and especially when I won't be able to fully understand it, no matter how hard I try.

In this anthology, I've collected a couple of my short stories of people having encounters with things much larger than themselves. These encounters leave them forever changed, often for the worse but sometimes for the better.

I've been calling this book a horror anthology while I've been working on it, but I'm not sure that description is accurate. For some stories, yes—you'll find flesh monsters and murderers and illicit medical experiments and more—but others are less horrifying and more fantastic. This, perhaps, underscores my relationship to the genre as a whole, that which truly scares me also transports me. That gut-churning fear sense always rides alongside the glory in the unlikeliness of our existence, and even when I try to write something purely scary, I always find my way back to somewhere transcendental in the midst of the blood and guts and tentacle beasts.

This is my first published book, and it's the culmination of a dream of authorship I've had since childhood. I'm thrilled to share it with you and I hope you enjoy.

- Simon, January 2023

KILLER

This story was first published in Kaleidotrope magazine in Autumn of 2022. It was my first ever publication credit (and first payment for a story... a whole $14!).

His hair was a burned-out green when we first met, the roots growing in dirty blonde. He had been scrolling on his phone, tugging at the shredded cuffs of his jean jacket, playing with his lip piercing, popping it all the way out of the skin and then sucking it in and making a deep dimple in the skin below his bottom lip. He told me he liked my tattoo, the sunflower peeking out from under the sleeves of my t-shirt. I smiled, asked about the patches on his backpack.

I had been drawn to him from the start, from the countless white-pink shiny lines of scar on his upper inner arms, from the way he did that smoky, too-much-eyeshadow thing and glared at the world over the waxed paper rim of his coffee cup, from the time I found the Percocet bottle from my surgery emptied after he'd left my place, from the way he scrolled through the heathered gray and pastel pink and tropical locales and LA backdrops of yoga influencers on his phone, his face pinched with a blunt animal longing for the myth of a clean, trouble-free life lived on porches in a perpetual sunset.

The incompleteness of him, the palpable pain and misery, and the way he threw himself into my care. "No one else understands me," he told me too many times to count, sounding like snippets from any teenage journal, his eyes big and wide and round like coins.

When he lied to me, and he lied to me often, there was a drawing-inward about him, an entirely unsubtle tell where his eyes would flick to my feet and his mouth would open only the smallest amount, as if he could escape his lie by barely saying it.

I craved these moments, moments where his shell cracked and I caught glimpses of the raw thing wriggling within and wondered about the thinness of its skin and how its spindly bones might snap like dry straw in a late summer wind.

He had been shy when he asked about it at first, which was strange since he'd been unabashedly kinky the whole time we'd been seeing one another. This was different to him, clearly, and it became clearer when the dam broke and the specificity of the fantasies came out. The brands (Wusthoff chef's, Cabela's deer-gutter), the settings (tied to a post in a shed while Eddie Vedder played on the radio, held face-down in a creek in the chill of late autumn), even the surrender of such details felt erotic in its intimacy. I listened with the air of concern appropriate to the situation and hoped he couldn't hear the blood that made the backs of my hands hot.

I agreed to try, but I set boundaries that tugged his expression into a frustrated frown: a dull knife, no gags, no restraints. That first time had been a disappointment for him, his eyes falling when I pressed the dull blade against his skin and it failed to leave anything but a slightly raised welt. It had been a disappointment for me as well, but I did not let that show.

I had been planning something like this in the abstract for years, you must understand, researching forensic technologies and anatomical details and learning, most of all, what oversights got people caught. I had a curiosity, born at a young age and nurtured by the small violences of rural living. It was a curiosity I was not necessarily determined to follow to its logical conclusion, but one that dogged me regardless and found ample space in my daydreams.

The eyes of a chicken, of a rabbit, they are always blown wide in a perpetual sort of fear from the moment you lift them to the point where they jerk in thunking, half-dead throes and the shininess goes out of their eyes. Their responses are mindless, nearly mechanical. But the eyes of a human, I thought those might hold more nuance. In this, I was not disappointed.

There is an art in this, but perhaps you cannot see it, and that is a shame.

I told him the gloves were for my protection. I told him we needed to take precautions, that blood-borne pathogens were no joke and that I would indulge him in this, but only if he indulged me in my concerns. He had laughed at this but allowed it.

His eyes broke first, those moon-gray irises blown wide with fear, and the tics of his skin, muscles tweaking nervously beneath flesh, and a certain trembling-between. A shudder towards and an immediate pulling-away as his body did what it could to protect him, though those reflexes were dulled from years of self-abuse.

It fascinated me, the way blood took a few moments to pool in the shallow cuts I left on his arms. I was particular in my cuts, following those guidelines written in scar, keeping only to angles plausible for self-infliction. I told him this was so he would not have to explain the marks to anyone else, though I am not certain my words meant anything to him at that point.

Will you believe me, then, when I tell you that he asked me to do it? That the shallow marks were not enough? That he ached for the blade to unearth those deeper arteries, the ones that spurted forth, taking us both by surprise, and me immediately thankful for the butcher's apron I'd worn to protect myself. We two watched the glutinous coagulation, not thin and watery at all but already sticking to itself, becoming tacky and clogging the drain and leaving a substantial thickness of ruddy red-brown in the tub.

Will you believe me when I tell you that he took my gloved arm and pulled it deeper?

Perhaps these are lies. You would have no way of knowing, really.

That night, the sky bruised brown and black, the machinations of a wildfire to end all wildfires out somewhere on the eastern slopes of the mountains. A windstorm contrived to blanket the sky in hazy darkness shot through with blood orange, almost neon, where the sun tried to break through. I walked the streets afterwards, feeling a high not unlike the purposeful near-madness of cocaine, not afraid of who might see me.

Reckless, yes. A mistake, but a harmless one in the end; everyone was outside, but all gazes fixated on the inexorable, dun behemoth in the sky that schemed to black out the sun.

A man on a rooftop blowing leaves out of his gutter with a leaf blower nearly lost his footing as a great gout of wind blasted through, staring as he had been at the cloud. Leaves and dust and little bits of trash kicked up. Hollow ponks marked the impacts of too-early buckeyes jarred loose by the wind striking carelessly parked cars, still in their spiky green shells. I waved to a family and their kids. They would hardly remember me when the world seemed so intent on ending itself around us. A spidery lightness trembled from the soles of my feet to the crown of my head.

When his roommate found him two days later, I confess I'd left town. I had fabricated an alibi for myself and it was airtight. I was suspected only in passing, as the partner always is in these matters, but even his friends came in to speak in my defense. I always made a point to court the friends; they would be indispensable if needed, and my care was worth the trouble as the police did not even question me as a suspect, as far as I could tell.

They did bring me in, but they mostly asked about his self-harm behaviors. The cops had his whole psych ward history spread there on the table, intakes and medications and years and years of therapy billed to insurance. I had been distraught, calling upon the skill I had practiced to summon tears. I rubbed my eyes red and puffy and raw. I gave conflicting answers and apologized. I gulped great sobbing breaths. They gave me tea and drove me home. The officer hugged me, man to man, patting me roughly on the back and mumbled some words of comfort.

It was a sadness, I am told, that he passed, but to me it was a revelation. The world now burned bright, full, profligate in its bounty, and the skies opened in rapturous downpour.

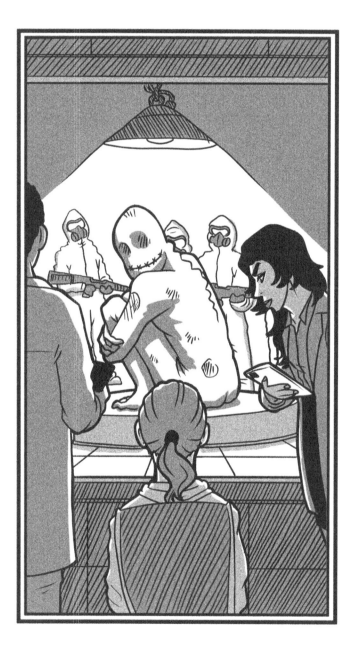

ANOMALOUS

Today they showed me the monster.

Taller than any person, it crouched on the center of the observation platform, lit from all sides by sterile lighting. A ring of bunny-suited techs surrounded it, rifles held at the ready. From behind, the knobs of its upper spine jutted out, ugly and raw against its ill-fitting skin. A patchwork of dead grays and irritated pinks and purples covered its nude form. Its long arms wrapped around its bony legs.

Its body faced away from me, but it had cranked its neck around to stare at me. The contours of its face flowed into one another too seamlessly. Its facial features were mostly shallow divots save for its grin, lips sewn together with leather cord, smile stretching the width of its blunted head.

"It's always looking at you regardless of where you are," said Dr. Sayeed. She held her stylus over her tablet, tapping the plastic with her nails. I swallowed, tried to think of something to say in return, and came up with nothing. I wondered whether my silence would make her suspect me more or less.

She'd had them run the standard tests yet again, watching for endocrine markers while I viewed the thing. They'd flashed some of the private words and scenes from my onboarding as a neural baseline. The adrenaline spiked, hot and cold on the back of my hands, when they dropped me into the recurring nightmare simulation of the dark attic strewn with broken toys, one blinking Hess holiday truck like a beacon of fear.

When they showed me the monster, the readouts remained neutral.

"Manifestations don't always appear the way you expect," said Dr. Diallo. "Remember, we're working with deep mind symbolism here. It could be something other than the form that connects it to you."

But they were grasping at straws. They couldn't tie the thing to me, and the thing had manifested with its mouth stitched shut, so it didn't seem inclined to tell them anything either.

Dr. Sayeed's impatience drew light furrows in her brown skin. It aged her more than her 40-odd years. She glanced at the thing, still staring at me through the one-way mirror, and then back at me. But whatever issue she had with me, there was only so much she could do about it.

They hadn't moved me out of the normal bunks, at any rate, so I was safe. Or safe enough.

"Is it yours?" asked Peggy.

"You know she won't be able to answer," said Dev with a frown.

I prickled at his chivalry. "She can answer for herself just fine," I said, and savored the way his gaze flicked to the table in discomfort. "And Dev's not wrong; I can't tell you anything like that. But what I can say is that I've never seen this thing before. I don't have any registered ghosts."

Peggy looked skeptical. "No *registered* ghosts. But come on, word's gotten around; it's always looking at you wherever you are. Fucking creepy. You sure that doesn't ring a bell?"

I sipped my coffee. "It could be someone else's. Someone who's obsessed with me." I glanced at to Dev, and he had the good grace to blush.

"Come on, Mik," he said.

"You know I'm just messing with you," I said. "But do you think I'd be sitting here with you if they thought it was mine?"

"Good point," said Peggy. "You sure it's not yours, Dev?"

He crossed his arms and rolled his eyes. "Check my registration," he said. "There's a big, fire-eyed dog-beast with knives for teeth, a talking cactus, and the zombie of my bitch of a grandma, not a weird, skinny Frankenstein."

During intake, they'd showed us images of the last large-scale manifestation. Ribs of rebar twisted through ravaged concrete flesh. Explosion scars from localized disturbances to the laws of chemistry. Building retrofits to accommodate the damaged curvature of spacetime. Stretchers and body bags. I hadn't believed them until they took us to the sub-basement and walked us through the space where gravity's vector skewed from the vertical, making us trip and fall one after another until we learned to hold ourselves at an angle to the ground. After that, I didn't know what I believed.

They assured us that a manifestation of that type was exceedingly unlikely, but reminded us that the best way to end one before it became a problem was to link it to its source. For us to let them know if we knew anything about anyone else in the cohort, things they might be hiding.

Manifestations happened all the time in the labs near where we worked with the doctors, apparently. Dr. Diallo had called it 'psychic out-gassing' when I'd asked him about it. Most lasted fractions of a second. They studied them with high-speed cameras.

The monster that stared at me had manifested three days before, though all it had done in that time was sit and stare and smile. Other people in the caf glanced at me, exchanged whispers. I stared at my breakfast and didn't say anything.

"Let's try this again," she said, her gaze hooking mine.

"Fine," I said, the leather of the restraints tugging against my wrists, pinching. The screen flashed in front of me, images too bright and brief to register, though I thought some of them might be bugs or animals. There were legs and fur. Maybe some numbers. My eyes watered from the glare.

"Do I need to be restrained for this?" I asked. "Dr. Diallo never restrains me."

"Dr. Diallo and I have different specialties," she said, as if this would explain. She glanced at the screen and smiled, and I could feel a blooming warmth in my chest at the small expression. I clamped down on it as fast as I could. I didn't trust her, I didn't like seeing her smile, and anything that pleased her was something I should probably be displeased by. More than anything, I just wanted to ignore whatever power game she was trying to play with me and get this session over with.

And it was easy enough to assume it all came from the circumstances. We had these sessions two or three times a week, and I was never really able to discern the purpose of them. We weren't allowed to talk about them after and were discouraged from even thinking about what had happened for our own sanity. This was the kind of thing they told us with a straight face, during intake.

The truth was, it wasn't easy to remember what happened in the one-on-one sessions. Peggy liked to make raunchy jokes about it, her with an outsize crush on Dr. Diallo—he did have a hell of a jawline—and the jokes helped us deal with the unease. Somehow it was less distressing to imagine her comical sexual-romantic scenarios unfolding than it was to think about what they might be doing to our brains.

She opened a big plastic jar, shaking it slightly with a look of displeasure at its near-emptiness, and then tipped the glittering shards of blue-white crystals into a crucible on her workstation. The crystals hissed slightly as they landed in the heated vessel, and twists of white steam emerged. The air smelled briefly of peppermint and hot metal. With practiced efficiency, she donned hot gloves and poured the liquid into the aperture on the machine by my side. After a few moments, the familiar tingly numbness returned to the skin around the IV in my arm, and spread throughout me until I felt like I laid in a bath of saltwater, perfectly suspended, at equilibrium.

"All right," Dr. Sayeed said, looking up. "Let's try something new. This time, I want you to say the first word that comes to your mind each time you see an image of a car."

"Can I have a drink of water first?"

She pursed her full, dark lips, and I wondered if she normally wore that bruise-purple lip color. She strode over slowly and took the Styrofoam cup from the metal tray next to me, her gloved hands squeaking against the sides. She lifted it to my face, not quite bringing the straw close enough for me to sip. I had to crane my neck, but I was thirsty and there was no fucking way I was showing this bitch that she was getting to me with her petty crap.

I swallowed, and she took the cup from me without asking if I was finished. "We'll continue," she said.

The images started to flash again, and I tried to focus on anything that looked like a car, but they were fast. I could barely catch more than a flash of any of them, and now I caught flashes of things more blush-inducing that the standard. Was that a pair of perky tits? Were those bodies wrapped sinuously around one another? Was it weird, to have noticed that they were paired sepia and peach, like Dr. Sayeed and I?

There was a flash of something red and enameled, certainly a car, something sporty, and I shouted "hot!" and then blushed to the roots of my hair.

Was that a flicker of a smile on her face? She said nothing, and the tests continued.

Nights after a session, I always found myself back in my bunk right after the caf closed for dinner, wrung out and fuzzy-brained. I tried not to worry about what was being done to me. Hell, I could only remember flashes of the session and they were fading fast.

The bunk cabin was small, enough space for my double cot, a small chest of drawers, a mirror, and a closet. There was a cabinet of a bathroom as well, the whole space sealing and converting into a shower. When I'd first arrived, I'd told the orderly that showed me around that it made me think of a luxury suite on a spaceship. The mattress was soft, memory foam, maybe, and with many thick blankets which I liked to ball up into a human-ish shape and sleep swaddled by.

On the chest of drawers, I had a framed picture of my dad. I kept it turned around since it wasn't easy to look at. When I'd first arrived, I'd had one of the lilies from the funeral too, but that had long since dried up and been thrown out.

I wished I could sleep. I kept shifting, feeling muscle twitches and tightness I couldn't account for. Peggy's nasty jokes about Dr. Diallo were sitting weird with me today. I'd had to ask her to stop, during dinner while she was describing the precise length and girth of his 'psychiatric qualifications'. I kept thinking of Dr. Sayeed's plum-purple lipstick.

Some deeper part of my brain suggested the sleep aid I might have if I let my fingers drift southward and do their magic, but I kept having these weird memories of what I'd been told about masturbation as a kid: how it was a sin, and how my dead Grandma who would always be watching me would know if I broke this particular rule of God's. And even if I didn't believe that stuff, even if I hadn't for years, the prospect of digging deeper into those feelings didn't appeal to me in the least. It wouldn't help me sleep, at any rate.

I picked up my journal instead and thought about writing. The last entry was from weeks before, though, and I hadn't written anything since the honeymoon feelings about this job had worn off.

Reading the last entry, my face grew hot with shame. I'd written it back when I'd thought this whole thing was an amazing opportunity, and I'd still felt special for having been chosen. Never mind the lack of explanation of what we were doing, never mind the lack of cell reception, hell, never fucking mind the impassible forest of fucked up crystal tree monsters and the prevarication when we asked to leave or communicate with the rest of the world.

It must have been so easy for them, driving me around in those unmarked black Cadillacs oozing quasi-governmental authority. I had been naïve enough to wink and nod along with them.

"Research," they'd said. They were seeking the "memetically gifted." And when you're fresh out of the funeral of the one person in the world who seemed to give a shit about anything in your fucking life, fresh out of a breakup with yet another worthless guy where things just don't fucking click no matter how hard you try, it feels good to be called "gifted". It feels great, really.

Back then, a three-month contract had sounded like nothing to me, even with the warnings that we'd be isolated for the whole of the time. I'd been more than ready to be cut off from a world that wanted nothing to do with me. It had sounded almost like a vacation. And once their advance had hit my bank account, and I'd been able to pay off the back rent I owed and then some, I'd thought I was a genius.

Now, I wondered if their timing in my life could have been that intentional.

I shut the journal with a snap that sounded angrier than I really felt, and let myself sink into a fitful approximation of sleep.

"Fuck you!" Peggy gasped, throwing the controller down in anger. "Fuck you."

I smiled grimly at her. I was never as good at these shooting games as my dad had been, but I had the muscle memory to be half-decent still. "Sorry," I said. "You're the one who wanted to go one on one."

"Yeah, well, I regret it now," she said, waiting for the ping of the respawn counter. "But I'll make you regret it soon enough." Her expression had gone petulant, and I tried to smile and screw up my brows into a game face, but I couldn't distract myself as easily as I usually could. There had been a few orderlies working their way through the lounge, cleaning, when we arrived, and as soon as they'd departed, a researcher had stepped in and taken a seat. She was far from us, but the timing had been too perfect for me not to notice. I'd come into the lounge with a vague desire to talk to Peggy, but the presence of these others spoiled that plan.

"God," she said. "It's bizarre that we get to just chill and game during the day. Some research project, huh?" But her tone was light, pleased, perhaps even joyful, sounding like a kid on a snow day.

"Yeah," I said, "it is weird."

The lounge was quiet this early in the day. We were allowed to keep whatever sleep/wake hours we wanted as long as we came in for our scheduled sessions and met the other lax medical and wellness requirements. A lot of people slept in. Hell, I wanted to sleep in after my sessions, too—there was something about leaning into the fuzzy, blank warmth of my mind on a day like today after a day like yesterday, with Dr. Sayeed and her lipstick, that was all too tempting. But something in my brain resisted the impulse to relax, and to let my guard down.

The lounge wasn't helping me, either. The space had the high-ceilinged look of a library, and the shelves around the perimeter were lined with all kinds of books and other media. Ditto, the computers and gaming consoles and TVs throughout the space that we were encouraged to use. There was plenty of space to relax, with squashy couches and beanbags. They encouraged us to spend time there, to go and unwind after the hard work we all did, but it was never quite acknowledged how all the media was local—none of these devices had network connections.

"Fuck!" said Peggy after I melee'd her from behind and she died again. "You bitch." Normally, her gaming temperament made me laugh. She was the picture of bland Midwest politeness at all other times, and had an impressive repertoire of words she could say instead of cursing. It was only deep in the competitiveness of shooting games where she dropped that act and showed some teeth. But today, I couldn't stop thinking about personality profiles and cohort planning, wondering how many of our interactions could be determined in advance.

"Say something," she said, turning her murder-face on me. "You don't get to thrash me like that in silence. It's creepy."

"Sorry," I said. But creepy was the right word for it.

"Mount up," said Dev with a grin through the open window of the hauler.

"You know procedure," said Dr. Diallo. "Roll it up, Dev."

He opened the passenger door and climbed in, and I got in the back. The seats of the hauler were bare bones, the thinnest fake leather covering with minimal padding, perfect for a quasi-military vehicle but not the comfiest for my bony ass, especially once we got moving off-road. I'd snagged a pillow from the lounge and put it down before I sat, hoping it would help. Dr. Diallo didn't notice, or didn't care if he did.

I hadn't been surprised to see Dev and I scheduled for a collection mission. Dr. Sayeed had been running low on crystals during our session the day before. Really, I was just thankful that we were going with Dr. Diallo rather than with her. Dev turned the hauler into the front parking lot and headed towards the checkpoint, and I was thankful to be off.

The campus we occupied was small, only a couple city blocks at most, and it was ringed in on all sides by the forest so you couldn't really miss it if you looked out any windows that faced the perimeter. I didn't really like to look at it, though. I don't think most people did.

The day dawned clear and bright, an early spring day that promised cool weather that might sweat you in the full sun. The sun glinted harshly off the blue-white facets of the crystal clusters that hung from all the tree-like shapes in the woods beyond. We called it a forest because that was the closest thing you could compare it to, but there wasn't any green in sight and there wouldn't be, even when high summer came on.

Dev pulled the hauler up to the guards at the checkpoint and we all flashed our IDs to their scanners. They did a sweep, looking under the chassis and in all compartments of the hauler and then waved us through.

"Where we headed?" asked Dev.

"About three quarters of a mile down we'll make our turn off," said Dr. D. "I'll let you know."

"What's the news from the higher-ups?" asked Dev. "Is that monster still staring at poor Mik?"

Dr. Diallo nodded. "While we're out, I'm having them correlate its head movements with our position. So far, they report a close tracking angle. But still no sign as to whose it is or what its purpose is."

"And you don't think it's Mik's?"

"Professionally, I withhold judgment," he said. "It's obvious why some people might think it would be hers, with the tracking and all, but it wouldn't be the first time we've seen a manifestation that focused on someone else when manifested by a person with an obsession, conscious or otherwise." He spoke in generalities, but there was an edge to his voice. If he wanted us to think he didn't have anyone in particular in mind, he failed. Dev flicked his gaze back to me in the rearview. "So we can't do anything until we know."

"Is there a procedure for figuring out who it belongs to?" Dev asked.

"We're doing our best, but this is the first time the manifestation itself hasn't been clear on who originated it. It's strange, how silent it is. Certainly a case study we'll be discussing for a long time."

"Is it dangerous?" I asked.

"It's contained."

An idea came to me; *it's contained, but not by them.* Did they know that?

"Right up here," said Dr. D, pointing to a trail off the main road. Dev turned, and the road went bumpy as shit and I was thankful for my cushion. The ground was rocky and barren, and every jolt made itself known to my rear, even through my cushion and the substantial hydraulics of the hauler. The earth was the rich black-brown of fertile humus where it wasn't rocks, but nothing whatsoever grew. Or nothing plantlike, at least.

Instead, surrounding us on all sides were the charcoal-black and twisted braids of the tree-things. Unlike normal trees, they didn't seem to grow as individual objects; the ground itself was covered in fibrous nets of thick, rootlike growths that we bumped over. In some places, they wrapped around one another and canted upwards towards the sky as if seeking the sunlight, but they had nothing on them to suggest they photosynthesized. They still took the form of trees, though, their banded arms wrapping together to form thick trunks and then branching apart into fractaled arms that spread wide like a crown. They certainly had a tree-ness to them, but the angles were all wrong, harsh and jagged rather than organic, and where there would be leaves they instead glittered with chunks of irregular, crystalline growths. They reminded me of those sticks of rock candy you could get at the fair.

"Just a bit farther," said Dr. D, looking at a GPS. "You won't miss our goal, I don't think, it's a big sucker."

Now that I was looking at the trees, I couldn't look away, but my brain was going sick-swimmy again. "Eyes out," said Dr. D, as if reading my mind. "We're almost there."

Dev whistled. "Big sucker for sure."

I looked out the windshield and, sure enough, it was obvious where we were headed, a massive tree, easily ten times the size of its neighbors. Where most trees in the forest had the size of a little sidewalk-sized maple in a city, this one was as big as a hundred-year-old maple growing alone in the center of a field, with a spreading crown just as wide around. The crystals in its branches fused at the tips, too, turning it into a big, glistening disco ball.

The first time I'd seen the forest, I'd thought it was beautiful and unearthly. I'd attributed the way my thoughts had become ungraspable and slick in my mind to the exhaustion of the journey to the compound.

Now, I knew better, and I turned away from its glittering threat as soon as I felt that floaty lightness come on. The effect of viewing the crystals wasn't nearly as strong as it was when we got them through the IV, but even the brief reminder of the session the day before was too much for me to handle.

"We'll have to be extra careful with this one," he said. "They get this big when a bunch of spikes fruit in the same location. It won't take long to get our sample, but I'll be extra susceptible when I turn back around to get into the car. Depending on where these ones are in their reproductive cycle, there might be increased hunting arm activity, so you'll need to be exceptionally aware."

"Can't you just keep facing it?" I asked. "Don't look back at us; keep your eyes on it and walk backwards?"

He shook his head. "Too dangerous; the washout will be strong with a tree like this. If I trip, it's worse than if you were guiding me. Dev, get us as close as you can."

Dev steered us in around the roots, which thickened into almost a pyramid around its trunk, all the winding, black angles netted together into an unholy plinth.

"The good news is that this one's heavy so I can reach the outer, fruiting branches from the ground."

Dev had cracked the top and he and I stood up into the sunroof, checking the plasma rifles. "You take this half," he said. "I'll take the other."

"You got it," I said, looking out into the woods. I kept the big tree in my peripheral, but as soon as I turned all the way to the right and it left my vision, my brain hiccupped.

Dr. D. must have noticed. "Don't turn all the way. It'll screw up your aim if you forget what you're looking for. Keep it in the corner of your eye; anything coming from that direction will come into your line of sight sooner or later, anyway."

I shivered. I'd never shot anything on a mission. Others had, but the rifles obliterated the targets, and the effect of the forest was such that even the shooters didn't remember what they'd seen. The phrase "hunting arm" brought to mind squids shooting out tentacles and suckers and barbs, deforming uncanny flesh over prey.

During intake, they'd warned us before they'd flashed images of damage from the arms, those massive, conical craters in faces, in chests. I'd peeked from behind my fingers at an image of a young man with an abdomen cored out in a neat oval. No one who had seen one could report accurately on their appearance, not with the effect from the crystals, but they embedded their form in the damage they did. That's why we called them crystal spikes. Most of the bodies weren't recovered, anyway.

"Ready?" asked Dr. D, pulling on the helmet of the Hazmat suit. I was under the impression it'd be less than useless if anything caught up with him.

"Ready," Dev and I said in unison.

Dr. D. popped the hauler door and set off for the trunk at a trot. He looked almost comical in the bright yellow suit. I looked away from him and out towards the glinting forest. The clear weather and bright sun made it hard to see past the glare on the crystal facets, but I kept my gaze beneath the trees, defocused to scan for movement. Sometimes, very rarely, it'd be a lost songbird, wandering in from the feeders near the campus.

"This branch will do nicely," called Dr. D. "Give me five minutes." He reached up, pulled the crystals towards him with a hooked metal pole, which he stuck into the ground, canting the arm towards him. It made a creaking noise less like wood and more like metal. The crystals clicked and clacked together, and the sonic hammer started with its peculiar high whistling sound as he started shaving off chunks and dropping them into his collection bag.

"Fuck," murmured Dev behind me. "I hate this part."

"Same," I said. I scanned my section of forest, the daylight a blinding blue. My stomach roiled, nauseous with fear.

They'd only given us the briefest description of what to watch for: any movement whatsoever in the forest, and we should shoot. There was no instruction given about what to do if we weren't armed.

"Almost done," called Dr. D. The branch he was shaving off looked nude without its crystal housing.

"Almost done," said Dev under his breath with the hint of a laugh. "Until the next time we go through this."

"Mm."

"Coming back now," said Dr. D. "I'm going to turn in three, two, one..."

"Dr. D," said Dev, slipping into the script like a pro. "We're right over here by the hauler. It's me, Devonte, and Mikaela is here too. You see us? Walk towards us, and keep a tight hold on the bag and tools you have in your right and left hands."

"Oh... all right," he said. Normally, he walked with a sense of calm purpose, but his stance now had a looseness to it. His expression had gone slack. Even though I'd been trained for it, his uncertainty sent a thrill of panic down my back.

"You got it, Dr. D," I said with the most encouraging smile I could manage. I was thankful that we were backlit by the sun, that he probably wouldn't be able to see the grimace that it really was. "Keep it up. We're right here."

"We're..." He hadn't stopped walking, but his gait was uneven, as he seemed to be trying to collect himself. "We're on a collection mission, yeah?" He made to turn his head.

"Don't look back!" called Dev. "Yes, collection mission. Nothing dangerous behind you; just a big-ass tree. If you look back, you'll feel the washout again."

"Ah," he said. "You never... really get used to this bit."

"Contact!" called Dev, and I heard the brief cough of his pulse rifle. I flinched hard, nearly turned before stopping myself.

"You got it, Doc," I said. "Dev's taking care of it. You just gotta keep walking here, and get back in the hauler. And don't drop the bag."

"Neutralized!" called Dev. "Fuck—wait!" Another rifle cough.

"Is... the door open?" asked Dr. D.

"It is. Almost there. You got it. What's going on, Dev?"

"Clear," he said, though he sounded uncertain. "Think I missed the first time. There was..." He audibly swallowed. "The root, there was a moving root. Something on the end of it. I don't remember." He shook his head hard, screwing up his expression as if that might jog his memory. "But I don't see anything anymore."

The sound of the hauler door unlatching and then slamming shut set my heart rate back to something approximating normal.

"Clear," I said, after a final scan, and Dev and I pulled ourselves back into the sunroof and he smashed the button to close it.

There was a moment of collective exhale.

Dr. D started pulling off the Haz-mat suit, looking at his haul. "Thanks, Mik. Thanks, Dev. This is an amazing sample, and that's a bitch-mother of a tree." He seemed to have returned to normal, with the tree in front of him again. I might've been stunned by his language if I wasn't feeling like I wanted to scream my own fucking lungs out. "Let's get the fuck out of here."

The lipstick was deep, clotted red today, almost burgundy.

"I thought I was supposed to work with Dr. Diallo," I said.

"He had a conflict. I'm covering for him," she said.

And what did it mean, watching her cinch the straps just to the edge of painful, that I didn't do anything to stop her? Was it that complex of heat that bloomed and burned in my gut, once I was restrained? The endorphins that coursed along the backs of my arms, my calves?

"Today will be a bit different," she said, face neutral, but there was something sparkling in her as well, some snapping tension that reflected and glittered in my own nervous system. My nipples grew taut against the cups of my bra and told myself it was from the cold. I wanted to rub against the restraints, to struggle, and I told myself it was because I wanted to escape.

I exhaled and closed my eyes. "All right," I said.

The screen flicked on and I flinched. It was the monster. It sat in the same position, hunched over itself in the center of the observation platform, lit from all sides.

"A live feed," she said. "It's looking directly at your current position."

I shivered. I tried to control my breathing, or at least to let my chest inflate past painful tightness. Then, the monster turned its head, and looked directly into the camera with its hollowed-out eyes, its empty grin.

Dr. Sayeed's eyes widened. "Interesting."

"It's not looking at me now?"

"That's a philosophical question," she said. "Now, let's begin. When you see a bicycle, I'd like you to say the first color that comes to mind."

Images flashed, half-seen in that moment and only barely recalled, as I recount this now. And were there more that seemed sexual, or was that just the errant heat in my thighs directing the images that I gravitated toward? My brain offered unhelpful observations and memories, surfacing them from the fog of our previous sessions. The length of her pencil skirt, and the way it rose above her knees when she bent down to adjust the machine, affording me a glimpse of the smooth skin of her thighs. The neckline of this blouse, deep enough to reveal a sliver of her bra beneath. The slowness of her gait as she circled me like a shark in the sea, her long brown legs sheened in black tights, slicing through the air, her black patent leather kitten heels clicking against the tiled floor. Her neutral expression, betraying nothing of what was going on behind her eyes, but still flushing me hot and cold each time she turned it on me.

My heartbeat ticked well above resting, my mouth dry, calling out strings of seemingly meaningless colors, then shapes, then days of the week, then holidays after watching brain-numbing sequences of imagery. The monster sat, staring straight at the camera with its loose grin. I would have thought it was a still image if it weren't for the occasional movement of researchers in the background.

Had it been an hour? Two? Perhaps more? The session room had no windows, and I flinched hard when Dr. Sayeed touched my shoulder before undoing the strap. Prolonged adrenaline activation left my body wrung-out, and I ached deep in my belly in this terrible, unsatisfied way that brought me back to the dark pit of night beside disappointing lovers, those men curled up soundly in their post-orgasmic slumber and me laying beside them feeling raw and worn out but somehow untouched, in some fundamental way. I wanted to cry, to scream, to get the thing out, this painful hardness lodged in my throat, under my nails.

Did she have to take her time with the restraints? Did she have to lean so low over me to get the calf straps, affording me the knowledge that her bra was made of thin, lacy stuff like lingerie and not a daily-wear cotton one? I was wet, and my brain wouldn't let go of the image of her leaning in after undoing the waist strap, hiking down my sweats and undies, and burying those lip-sticked lips between my legs.

No fucking wonder, of course. I hadn't gotten laid in the weeks I'd been on campus. No fucking wonder I'd turn something clinical like this into something more. No fucking wonder I'd be thinking about this with a woman; I was straight as an arrow, straight in the most standard and boring kind of way, and it would really take sexual deprivation to make me think this way. Wouldn't it?

The monster in the feed moved, just slightly. It leaned forward an inch or two. Its grin might've widened. The look of a kid watching a movie, naked anticipation on the face of the protagonist at the emotional climax of things. I resented the expression and its implication. There was nothing to realize here.

She'd finished with the straps, and she straightened up, tugging the edge of her pencil skirt down.

"Enjoy the rest of your day," she said.

I sat behind a hedge, my feet flat on the ground and my back up against the painted cinderblock of building 3.

I couldn't fully account for why I was here; part of that was the effect of staring at the forest, and the rest was probably whatever the fuck Dr. Sayeed had done to me in that session. I couldn't remember, other than that I'd felt like I needed air afterwards, after whatever all those flashed images of sex had been. Why did I remember what underwear she was wearing? I kept my eyes trained on the distant line of trees, enjoying the sensation of weird, swimmy blankness.

"...doesn't justify breaking procedure," said a voice I recognized, some doctor I didn't work with. From the way she pitched her voice down, I knew immediately I was overhearing something meant to be private. "And, in fact, we've learned nothing. Breaking procedure means that we can't be certain of disentanglement. Beyond the ethical concerns, which are distressing to an extreme, this has proven exactly nothing."

"I'm struggling to believe this myself," said Dr. D. in a low voice. The two of them came into view around the corner, walking slowly. He had to lean his head down slightly towards her since he had a solid foot of height on her. I hoped they wouldn't see me, but I didn't think they would. I was in the shadow of the building, sitting in the dirt somewhere you wouldn't expect anyone to be, and they were clearly wrapped up in their discussion. "It wasn't even that long ago that we were fighting about line items on the entry, exit, and washout list. Wasn't she the one that wouldn't let go of the importance of avoiding memkeying and transference? And now..."

"Yeah," said the other doctor. "Well, you'll perhaps be glad to know I've taken her off all caseloads for now."

"What did you put on the form?"

"Personal entanglement," she said. "She'll hate it, and she'll fight it, but I'm Director and even if she fights and wins, it gives us a little time with her on the bench."

"Are you sending her home?"

"No," she said. "She's an old friend. I know a little of what's going on back home for her, why she might be acting out like this. It doesn't excuse anything, but I want to keep her around here. Take her off cases for now, let her relax for a bit. Believe me, the facilities here are a lot nicer than what she has to go home to."

"What about Mikaela?" asked Dr. D, and I started, thinking for a moment that he'd seen me, but they were moving past me, facing away from me.

Yeah, what *about* me, bitch? You've got all this pity for your friend and her medical malpractice, but what about the one suffering because of it? My stomach bloated with rage.

"I'll move her case to you as primary, if you're good with that."

"Sure," he said, "but are you worried? If Aya is still staying local?"

"Of course not," snapped the doctor. "She'd never do anything—well, nothing beyond what she's already done."

And I could hear the wavering there, sure, that necessary lying to one's self to protect the image you have in your head of a person. And even if I understood it, I felt nothing but helpless anger and fear.

I knocked as gently as I could on Dev's door.

"You up?" I murmured.

There was some muffled sound of movement and the door cracked open, but only enough to show half of his sleepy face and the brass glint of the door chain. "'sup Mik?"

"I need to talk to someone," I said, and my brain clicked into the track of interaction with men that was worn deep in my mind. I looked down, I flickered my lashes prettily. I had no interest in Dev, but I felt this magnetic tug to the roleplay, this thing I was supposed to be doing. I'd felt weird grabbing the condoms, too, but there was a strong sense of duty surrounding my inhabiting this role and I had no energy to investigate it further.

He looked concerned. Maybe a little horny, but also wary, and I realized some part of me saw the intimacy script as a way to get around that barrier. If I'd had any emotional bandwidth left, I might've hated myself for going along with it. "It's Dr. Sayeed."

The mutual dislike worked its magic more than the halfhearted sexual overtures had. He undid the lock and ushered me inside fast. He sat on the bed, and motioning towards the one chair he had in the room. "Tell me about it."

When I sat, I could feel the rubbery circles of the condoms under my ass in my pocket and I could have laughed. Sitting here with Dev, him handsome as all hell and coming on strong with those concern and care vibes and not a shred threatening, and both of us probably perpetually undersexed for weeks, months maybe, I thought to myself that if I was gonna want a man, this would be the moment. But nothing could have been further from my mind.

"Dr. Sayeed has it out for me and I don't know what to do," I said.

He leaned back. "Yeah," he said. "She sure does. You worried she's gonna try something?"

"She already has," I said, and my mouth went tacky-dry because saying this meant admitting to myself that she had already fucked with me, and I didn't even fully remember what had happened. "They took her off my case. I'm with Dr. D. now. But I dunno, man, I still don't feel safe. She's still here. I have no idea what I expect. It'd just be nice to feel like I had some backup."

"Have you talked to anyone in charge? Dr. D, maybe?"

"They won't do anything about it," I said. The director seemed disinclined to see her friend as a threat, and I didn't feel like confessing my fears to some lady whose first thought had been to protect her friend over the person she'd harmed.

"I'm not surprised," he said, and I realized that the distrust that made us so wary around one another could invert and bond us, too.

He planted his feet on the floor and then leaned towards me, his eyes narrowed. "What can I do to help, Mik?"

...

She was already in the passenger seat and Dev was forcing himself through painful small-talk when I climbed into the back, a distant part of me realizing I'd forgotten my cushion, another distant part acknowledging that she'd never have let me keep it with me. She'd rather see me suffer, wouldn't she?

Somehow, I hadn't been surprised at all to see her name on the hauler schedule for today. The change had been last minute, and since the Director hadn't done shit to protect me, there was no official sanction against us doing a non-psychological job together. I'd pointed it out to Dev over breakfast, and though there hadn't been a chance to have a private conversation about it, I could see he saw the potential danger too.

"Yo, Mik," said Dev, with a significant look at me. "You ready?"

"Let's go," I said.

Dr. Sayeed did not acknowledge my presence in any way whatsoever. I was thankful for Dev's lighthearted chatter that he kept up even as Dr. Sayeed said nothing. I suppose that's how he dealt with nerves.

We made it through the checkpoint nearly without a hitch, though I saw the looks the security people gave to Dr. Sayeed. "Check the schedule, if you're concerned," she snapped at them, and they did, and somehow that didn't help me feel any more comforted.

"Where're we headed?" asked Dev.

"Six miles down," she said. "I'll tell you when to turn."

I kept my eyes glued to the forest, drinking it in, letting it fill my field of vision. The numbing sensation from the trees lulled me. The ride was interminably long, and after a while, even Dev lapsed into silence. I was thankful when Dr. Sayeed said, "turn here."

Yet another fucking crystal tree in yet another samey-looking bit of this cursed landscape. Rage sparked inside me at everything, at having to pretend this was normal. At Dev, even, for trying to make things seem okay with his forced cheer.

"All right," said Dev, as he parked the hauler. "Mik and I are old hands at this, so you get suited up and we'll check the rifles."

"Actually," she said, "Mikaela's going to retrieve the sample. I'll handle the rifles with you, Devonte."

"I don't think so, doc," said Dev, and there was challenge in his tone. Had I resented him before, for standing up for me? In this moment I still did, but I resented myself more, for not standing up for myself. "We're not trained to collect. We know how to work the rifles, and that's it."

"She'll be fine," said Dr. Sayeed, reaching into a compartment and fishing out the Haz-mat suit and then tossing it back to me. I caught its soft weight without a word. I wanted to say something, anything, but the words wouldn't come. "She's got *oodles of team spirit*." She said this last bit with weird emphasis, and as the last syllable left her mouth, my muscles went a tiny bit slack. It wasn't just the trees, though it reminded me of their effect, a sense of complacency, a lessening of resentment. A body memory of deference, and the safety in obedience.

And with that complacency rode anger. I would have to obey her, and I resented it. I was a kid again, getting told I would have to go to trumpet lessons yet again, despite the fact that I hated the instrument, hated the thing I had to do with my lips, hated my instructor who treated me with such disdain when I couldn't make any sound but a feeble honk. It was sadness and anger and a sense of helplessness, and more than everything it was the knowledge that there was nothing I could do about it.

It wasn't until I saw Dev's body language go loosey-goosey as well that I realized it was a fucking weird phrase for her to have said. It was something memetic, I realized, and that realization gave me something to grip onto in my own mind even as my arms started unfolding the suit.

"I don't..." Dev was struggling. He gripped the steering wheel. He glanced at me in the mirror. Even though my arms seemed intent on pulling on the bunny suit, and even though there was a sense in my mind of the floaty pleasure in listening to her, there was enough left of me to catch his glance to the door and then back at me.

I nodded, and he changed, went slightly slack. "All right," he said, and accepted the rifle I handed him.

I had a thought, then, that Dr. Sayeed was one of the most beautiful women I'd ever seen, and something peeled back enough for me to get my hands under my own control again.

"Doc, what's this?" Dev asked, showing her something on the clip of the rifle he was inspecting. She leaned towards him to look, and I leaned forward and unlatched the door and shoved it open. And in a flash, he had grabbed her by the shoulders and pushed her.

She went tumbling out the door nearly head over heels. He reached over to pull the hauler door shut and snap the lock, and then seemed to release some tension in him and go limp.

And I understood; as soon as he fell back against the chair, and as soon as the doors were locked, that soft, fuzzing wave of memetic suggestion swamped me, wanting me to continue putting on the bunny suit and wait for further instruction.

I woke in complete confusion. I could not understand what these strange trees were, nor what that muffled banging sound could be, but the hard angles of the military transport framed my world, pierced with the gold of the sunset that streamed through the windshield.

"Mik," said a voice, Dev, and I snapped into the present, my head lifting from where I'd rested it against the glass like a kid falling asleep on a long car trip. I looked out the window and saw the source of the sound.

Dr. Sayeed banged on the glass of the hauler, her face pressed against the window, contorted in fear. Then, movement, and my brain barely had enough time to process what was happening when I realized something angular and black hung behind her. She screamed, and the bulb of the thing inched over her shoulder, turned, lifted like a vine, and extruded a glistening black spike from a wrinkled sheath of bark-like flesh. Then, her head snapped back, and I turned away.

"Let's go back," said Dev. "Let's get medical." As if this wasn't something we'd done on purpose. To cover for us, or to let him imagine we hadn't just killed her?

"Let's go back," I said.

It was dark, but as he turned, the headlights washed over the roots before us. I caught a flash of motion, not enough to resolve with precision but enough for my brain to register the unwelcome verb 'peeling'.

"We could go," I said. "We could take the hauler and get the fuck out of here."

"Limited range," he said. "With the charge we have left, we won't make it even halfway down the access road. They only charge 'em with enough for the mission, plus a bit of slop. We could try, but then we'd be in the middle of the forest without anything to do but wait for someone to pick us up."

"Figures," I said, as he turned back towards the campus.

I hadn't figured out what I was going to say when we got back, but when we returned, we didn't have time to explain anything.

"Mik, observation room now," said Dr. Diallo as soon as we'd stepped out of the hauler, and I went.

"It's agitated," he said. "It's been crying and clawing at itself ever since you left. We thought you might be in danger."

"Dr. Sayeed," I said. "She got hurt, in the forest."

He nodded. "Medical is speaking to Devonte already. This work affects people in all kinds of ways. Accidents happen." He said this with a significant look at me. "I want you to put whatever happened out of your mind. You are not at fault."

"I..." I swallowed. "Thanks."

So he knew. Some part of me wanted to be thankful he seemed to be letting us off the hook, but mostly I just felt rage, that he'd known and he'd done nothing.

Everyone in the crowded observation room stepped away from the metal chair in the center when I arrived and stared at me. Conversations died, and a flush crept into my cheeks. I sat in the chair and looked at the monitor.

If the monster had been distressed before, it looked calm now, though I could see red welts on its arms and sides where it had scratched itself. Though I didn't know the thing, my heart ached for it, to see how it'd hurt itself.

There is something wrong with me, whispered some little shard of me, from deep within the tangles of my mind.

The monster's head stretched back. Its jaws strained against the laces that held its mouth shut. It brought its dirty nails to its sides and scratched frantically.

"What's it doing?" demanded one of the techs, leaning towards the one-way glass.

I deserve what happened to me. What she did. Because I asked for it.

The air in the observation room filled with a grating whine. "That's the sound it's making," said Dr. Diallo. It sounded like cold, late nights, crying outside by the locked front door of the house, wishing for sleep. It sounded like the high whine of surveillance, the constant monitoring of word and expression and glance, the driving need to be perfectly palatable, to hide the undesirable so deeply that even *I* might remain unaware. Tears filled my eyes. *I asked for this because I wanted it. I wanted it because there's something wrong with me.*

"Turn it off," I said, and Dr. D killed the audio feed. Everyone glanced away from me.

I wanted her to do it because I'm gay.

The monster reached its gnarled fingers towards and then, sickeningly, into the orbit of its eye, and plucked it out without flinching. It crushed the eye within its large hand. All of the researchers leaned towards the observation window.

The monster fished something out of the remains. A tiny key, glinting silver in the light, like something from a child's diary. It raised a finger to its lips, looking at me as always. The expression it wore, something that looked like a jack-o'-lantern melted into November, stayed the same, but there was something playful about it.

I'm gay, I thought again, and the idea swelled within me, full color and expansive. The charcoal sketch of fear that had caged it, the part that whispered that I'd been abused by this desperate person as a result of this unacceptable detail of myself, dissolved like a shred of smoke into the daylight of my understanding. No matter how I had come to this truth about myself, the truth washed over me, clean and bright.

Despite myself, I smiled back.

"What does it have?" called one of the techs. "Drop it, now!"

But it was fast, faster than them by far. I couldn't see what it did with the key, but it didn't really matter; locks and keys were a matter of physical reality and this was a memetic manifestation, something that existed in idea more than in form. The key likely manifested as a concept our brains could understand. It showed us the key, not because it needed to use it to escape, but rather to show us that it was already beyond our reach.

It de-manifested, leaving behind a curious visual negative for a few moments.

Tears still streamed down my cheeks, but their warmth was the lapping edge of an ocean of memories—kissing the neighbor girl, that doll I'd called my girlfriend, the Victoria's Secret catalogs I'd hidden in the drawer with my petticoats. I couldn't stop myself from smiling. It was a benediction, a blessing, a soft wash of forgiveness and light.

Somewhere distant I heard shouting, the strange rattle of anti-memetic weaponry. With forgiveness came holy fire, I guess. But it didn't matter much to me; I was free.

DUE SOUTH

Every town Jacob had passed through had been intact but abandoned.

Earlier in the day, he had perused the ransacked shelves of a grocery store that, though crisscrossed with muddy footprints, still bore construction paper cutouts of leaves and pumpkins on the windows facing the deserted parking lot. Autumn had come and gone, and the air smelled like snow.

Crows called to one another in the trees, and he buttoned his coat. He had an idea of the number of miles that stretched before him, but only a rough idea of how quickly he could travel them. He wondered whether he would reach Florida and Adrian before winter reached him.

Day had dawned hours before, but the flat gray-white of the clouds above had smoothed the sunrise into something drawn-out and timeless. The deserted interstates were hypnotic in their quiet without the far-off singing of tires on pavement. He found comfort in the silence. He traveled along I-95, now somewhere south of Richmond, far from the shattered husks of beltway buildings where he had hoped and feared to find others. But there had been no one.

The only sounds were the dry rattling of the wind through bare branches and the harsh calls of jays. How far to Jacksonville? He did not know.

Jacob had always been the good kid.

Brothers they may have been, but stood next to one another you'd have to look pretty hard to see a resemblance between the two of them. Jacob had been most comfortable at rest behind a book or computer screen, but sitting still had always chafed against Adrian's sharp edges. Where Jacob found pleasure in unassuming style and a life lived within familiar patterns, Adrian dressed in black denim and studs and threw himself against the rules until they broke, unafraid of parents and police alike.

Adrian's rebelliousness had earned their mother a substantial Xanax prescription so she could keep her panic attacks under control. Adrian stole pills and snuck cheap beers from the fridge when it had been full enough for a few cans to go missing unnoticed. He made a habit of sneaking back in through the garage just before dawn, slipping under the half-open door.

Adrian used to call him a wuss for wanting to stay home and play video games while he got up to whatever it was he was getting up to at night, and he'd hated Adrian for making him feel like a loser. For as hard as Adrian pushed himself not to conform, Jacob had pushed himself to excel in academics and had earned the title of "the good kid" as a result. The title highlighted the gap between them, pushed them further apart.

To no one's particular surprise, Jacob secured a full ride to U. Penn to study biomedical engineering while Adrian had dropped out a month before graduation. They did not speak for the four years Jacob was in college and he didn't allow himself to admit that he worried about his brother. Ever since middle school he'd felt a distant hatred and fear worrying the edge of his consciousness, and as Adrian had gotten stick-and-pokes and started snorting pills with ferocious glee, he had come to understand the fear was not his but Adrian's, somehow staining the edges of him. All through college in the deep of night, he'd feel the hem of it, muddied, toxic, and drowning.

He went home for Christmas every year, but Adrian never showed up. He didn't speak his brother's name around his parents, especially not around his mother. The Christmas after graduation when he brought Zara home to meet his parents, when he told them he intended to marry her, his father remarked it was a shame that Adrian wasn't there to share the news. His mother said nothing but drank two bottles of wine. He'd heard her sobbing wetly in the living room at night when he woke to use the bathroom.

Jacob's pack crinkled with the metallic wrappers of granola bars and trail mix. He wouldn't be able to subsist indefinitely on snack foods, but for the time being he had little energy to put towards anything beyond scouring grocery stores and convenience marts for shelf-stable foods until he made it farther south.

The days grew noticeably colder.

...

Their wedding was going to be a simple affair at her parents' lake house in North-Central Pennsylvania, and Zara had gently suggested that Adrian would be welcome if Jacob felt comfortable inviting him.

Jacob had not spoken to his brother in seven years. He still had "Adrian" listed in his phone. He had no idea if the number was still his, but one April day when the sun burned hot and the shadows chilled, he pressed call.

The call connected, rung once, twice, and then cut to voicemail. Ignored. He nearly dropped his phone in his haste to end the call before it recorded a message. A group of robins in a nearby tree descended to the grass in front of his house all at once. He wanted to throw his phone on the ground.

Instead, he swallowed and called again. Conscious of the dryness of his mouth, he waited for the robotic voice to provide him with the instructions to leave a message.

"Hey, Adrian. It's me. I know it's been a while." His voice stuck for a moment on the magnitude of this understatement, his head swirling with explanations and apologies and years of unvoiced feelings.

He swallowed and continued, "I'm getting married. Her name is Zara, and she's wonderful. You're my brother, and I want you to be there. The wedding is in June. June 18th. So, uh, call me back. If you want. Hope you're doing okay."

Minutes later, he'd felt the hem of his brother's thoughts surge against his, ringing with the metallic tang of regret.

...

Jacob made camp west of the blurred gray line of the Atlantic. The landscape had given way to unfamiliar marsh plants and an organic, loamy smell of ground that was yet unfrozen. The mornings had ceased to coat the outside of his tent with frost, but he built a fire anyway with the driest of the mossy wood that he could find among the twisted marsh trees. The logs smoked and coughed before igniting.

The brushing of his brother's thoughts against his had grown more insistent, now a constant hint of presence rather than intermittent flashes of strong emotion. In moments of idleness, his eyes would wander to the south, but the sense of purpose that crowded him while he traveled would lose ground to the loneliness in the evenings. He pushed himself all the harder during the days to welcome sleep as soon as the sun set.

In his exhaustion, he did not stop to examine the borders of the marshland. He permitted himself not to consider why the water looked clotted, thick, unevenly colored. An acrid, unwashed-body sort of smell hung in the air now, and, unfamiliar with the territory, he allowed himself to imagine this was simply the smell of southern marshlands and left it at that.

Adrian hadn't called or come to the wedding, but three days into their honeymoon in Croatia, Jacob received a text message.

"congratulations. miss you"

The rest of the trip, he would pull his phone out and open the message, reading and re-reading it. Laying in bed with the soft warmth of Zara pressed up against his back, he would stare at the text and begin typing a response only to delete it, emptied of words.

Nearly a month later, still forming unsatisfactory messages in his head and discarding them, Adrian called him.

Jacob picked up. "Hello?" he asked, immediately forgetting every conversation he had rehearsed.

"Jake?" Adrian's voice sounded cracked, thicker, somehow.

"Yeah."

"Hey."

A pause. Nearly eight years of silence hung between them. Jacob licked his lips, trying to figure out what he could possibly say.

"Congratulations on your wedding," Adrian said, voice slurring and slow. Adrian's heart sank. "I'm sorry I didn't make it."

"That's all right," said Jacob. "We would have loved to have you there, but I know it's difficult." The words he wanted to say crowded to the front of his mind, but he was afraid to say anything, afraid he'd shatter this fragile thread connecting them.

He heard a snuffling and realized that Adrian was crying, and he blinked as his own eyes blurred with a warmth of tears. "I need help," Adrian said. "Jake, I'm in a bad way and I don't know what to do about it."

"Anything, Adrian. Where are you?"

"In Philly," he said.

"I'll be there in three hours," he said. "I'll call you."

The air grew humid by degrees, and the signs over I-95 ticked down the miles to Savannah with painful slowness. Pride ballooned in his chest when the count dropped to single digits, but it settled like indigestion next to the unexplored knowledge of the madness of his journey. Had he really walked all this distance through emptied towns?

Questions such as this were for ignoring, as they would rob him of his purpose long before he found his brother.

Despite the lack of human presence, the evidence of people remained. The roadsides crowded with parked and abandoned cars, and a confusion of footprints turned the grass beside the highway into imprints of mud. Many of the car doors he tried were unlocked, and a few had supplies in the seats. He refilled his water bottles and food caches. Tree limbs hung heavy, thick with what he made himself believe was southern swamp moss. Flies buzzed and the smell of decay thickened the air.

The part of his mind that belonged to Adrian pulled him ever onward, like a distant sound that compelled him to approach so he might hear it clearly.

He had never told anyone what it had been like when he found Adrian.

His brother had been at the brink, in a dank and terrible place. When Adrian saw that Jacob had come for him, he broke down in hitching sobs. His face was unwashed, unshaven, skeletal.

Jacob hauled him to his feet and brought him to a hotel room and laid next to him the entire night as he shook and puked. Only later did he learn how lucky he was that nothing worse had happened that night, and hours later his brother was in a hospital as the withdrawal started in earnest.

It had probably been around then that the red tide had become national news. Headlines had been almost laughably tabloid-esque in an era of one pandemic after another, all-caps statements about flesh-eating parasites and connective tissue dissolution. It was one more biblical plague to add to the list, and Jacob had filtered it out in those early days, so preoccupied had he been with his brother's recovery.

As he passed into the outskirts of Savannah, the Adrian-presence in his head swelled out from the edges of his thoughts and into the meat of them, blending with those that came from his own mind.

The city was as silent as a photograph, but the river breathed, edges clotted with something thick and organic. The stench near the water, that same sour rankness of body odor, made Jacob cough.

He ventured into stores looking for supplies and found the air close and humid, more humid even than the air outside. He was well within the CDC's cordon, and Jacob let that knowledge pass through his mind without purchase. If he stopped to think about what he was doing, he would never make it to Adrian.

He let the stuffy buildings lie and instead gathered what supplies he could from cars along the highway that were free of any biological material.

Memories of those brief days in the winter and early spring after his brother's exit from rehab were painful in their brightness, now.

Introducing Zara and Adrian and seeing the ghost of his suave teenage bravado as he playfully flirted with her. The blanched look on Adrian's face as Jacob pulled his car into their parents' driveway. The equally stunned expressions they wore, framed by the sliding front door's frame. Tears, laughter, shouting, more tears. The entire family together for the holidays for the first time in nearly a decade. The rapturous look on Adrian's face when he accepted the tiny baby Christopher into his arms for the first time.

As life settled into regularity, as Christopher crawled and then toddled and walked, as Adrian found himself work as a mechanic and came to Jacob and Zara's every Sunday for family dinner, a contentment settled over Jacob. His brother's emotions still passed by his own in his mind, but they were without their jagged edges, and he was glad.

But at dinner, Adrian would usually have a few more beers than Jacob was comfortable with before driving home. And sure, his apartment was three miles away through neighborhood streets, and sure, he knew his brother knew his limits, but he worried. And little by little, those thoughts of his brother's that hung on the edge of his own consciousness clouded over and darkened.

Zara had mentioned her own concerns about Adrian's drinking and Jacob had responded in denial and anger. He burned with shame, remembering the things he'd said to her in his brother's defense. He had been afraid to consider that his brother might be falling away from them again. After that, she had stopped bringing it up, and after the minor accident that led to Adrian's DUI that had happened on the way home from dinner, she stopped the dinners as well.

...

The highway south of Savannah clotted with cars, some spilling off the sides, most now bearing some sort of fleshy growth around the tires and sometimes dotting the interior. His hiking boots squelched through the swampy earth. Adrian's presence in his head roared dully, grinding through his exhaustion and tugging him south. Pinkish clouds hung heavy in the sky overhead. A rhythmic sensation of air pressure changes now surrounded him, as if the wetlands were breathing.

He and Zara hardly spoke about Adrian after the DUI, and they saw less and less of him. On the occasions when Jacob did see his brother, they met in loud, dark bars where Adrian drank heavily. Jacob always insisted on giving him a ride home, but couldn't bring himself to acknowledge the extent of his brother's drinking beyond that.

Monica, the girl Adrian had been seeing, broke up with him. Adrian's job performance suffered, and the owner of the garage fired him. And one wet spring day, when he pulled into his brother's apartment complex after a week or so of radio silence, he found Adrian's apartment empty.

Angry and desperate, he called his brother. Adrian didn't pick up. He called twice more and left a message, demanding to know where he'd gone, all his suppressed concern spilling out of him in white-hot rage. He couldn't bring himself to talk to Zara about what had happened. He couldn't acknowledge that he'd known something was wrong and that he'd failed to do anything about it.

A call came nearly two months later, not from Adrian, but from a hospital in Jacksonville, Florida. His brother had checked himself in to a detox program and had listed Jacob as his emergency contact. He would be unable to speak to Adrian until he was further along, but they let him know that his brother was safe and getting the help he needed.

There was something fitting about it. Adrian had always run from his problems. This time, he'd nearly run off the edge of the map.

By the time he was only a few days from Jacksonville, the landscape had transformed.

The ground pulsed with a thick slurry of grayish-brown organic matter that sucked at his soles. He put on two pairs of pants, one over the other, and tucked the ankles into his boots. The stuff festooned the trees around him like fleshy garland. That unwashed smell was so constant that Jacob had long since stopped smelling it. There was something decayed looking about the trees as well, with great chunks that seemed to be sloughing off.

Adrian's presence had become a constant companion to him, a mute presence in his brain yanking him along farther and farther south. He didn't spare much thought for anything beyond the necessities of survival, rationing what food he had and finding safe places to sleep.

Adrian was still alive in this terrible wasteland, and Adrian was all he had left. He'd allowed his brother to drift away before. He wouldn't allow that to happen again.

...

The panic that had finally set in when the CDC announced a quarantine of the Southeastern shore of the country washed over the country seemingly all at once, uncertainty curdling into terror in the wake of news reports bracketed with warnings of the disturbing nature of the images within.

Highways were shut down and the National Guard patrolled the woods, first capturing and later shooting on sight those who tried to flee on foot. News outlets, followed by entire towns, dropped from contact. Atlanta and Charlotte canceled all flights. What news did escape was unbelievable. Nothing even approximating a cure existed. All that could be done was to try to keep it contained and let it burn itself out.

Life continued, but everyone was stretched to their breaking points, especially those with family and friends somewhere in the cordon. People kept picking up and heading south to look for their loved ones.

"What the hell is wrong with them?" Zara had demanded as yet another of her coworkers put in their notice. "There's a quarantine for a reason, and the National Guard is shooting anyone who tries to get through either way. I don't know what they're thinking."

Jacob agreed with her, but in his heart, he ached to drive south. He could still feel Adrian and he knew there would come a point where he wouldn't be able to stand it any longer.

Zara had lapsed into a tight-lipped silence about the inexplicable migration, and one morning, when Jacob had made up his mind to leave, Zara surprised him by leaving first. She packed Christopher into their old station wagon and, with only a brief word to him, said she was going to find her family who had fallen out of contact along with their town in South Carolina.

He stood in the driveway that afternoon, late summer sun blazing against the skin of his neck, staring at the empty garage. He braced his body for the icy crush of panic and fear that he knew would come, watching his wife take their child into the heart of whatever horrors awaited them in the south, but no such feeling arose. In its place, he found that steely sense of purpose, that magnetic draw to the south, and he thought only of his missing brother.

At the time, he had considered this a blessing and thought no more deeply of it.

He entered Jacksonville in the early morning, sometime before the sun had risen. The skies had taken on a uniform and dirty pink coloration somewhere in Georgia and the weather hadn't changed since, but they grew marginally lighter when the sun rose, bathing the ground below in a peachy, diffuse daylight that cast no hard shadows.

The streets were thick with vehicles of all types, spilling off into the ditches on the side of the road. They were all parked, most with doors ajar, as if a crowd had come clamoring to the city, but he had seen no one. He hiked into the heart of the metropolis, trying to avoid the thickest clumps of the stuff that coated the ground and climbed the sides of the buildings.

The smell was thick enough to taste, and the humidity made him sweat through his shirt. The sun burned somewhere behind the dull clouds. Adrian tugged him onward almost painfully, his head feeling swollen with his brother's presence. He had to work to pull his boots free of the thick sludge with each step.

The hospital doors were fixed ajar by the fleshy growth. The exterior of the building was skin like and pulsing. His stomach churned at the sight, but he steeled himself and entered.

"Adrian?" he called. "It's Jacob!"

The fleshy matter coated the interior and the waiting room looked more like the interior of a living creature than of a building. Thick veins bulged along the walls and visceral masses pulsed in the shadows. His voice died just feet in front of him, sucked into the walls.

He took a deep breath and shouted, "Adrian!"

The Adrian in his head jerked him forward, and he gasped as his legs seemed to spill him onward of their own accord. He moved through an opening that had once been a door but now opened like an iris of skin. He pulled a flashlight from his pack and flicked it on. The light bounced off the slick flesh that surrounded him, and pockmarks pinched shut like rudimentary eyes wherever he shone his light. He stepped carefully over the drum-tight translucence of what looked like a stomach full of some unspeakable liquid. Jacob gagged, his mouth filling with spit.

"Adrian!" he shouted.

"Jaa...cob." His brother's voice emanated from the space in front of him, strained and weak. He shined his flashlight around the cavity.

"Adrian! I'm here!" He stepped forward, only to fall. His feet were stuck fast in the organic matter that surrounded him and had begun to creep up his ankles. He could feel its warmth seep into his shoes. "Fuck!" he cursed, dropping his flashlight. He reached out his hands to grope for it, adrenaline ringing at the backs of his eyes and the migraine of his brother's thoughts bearing down on his brain. The flesh beneath his hands was warm and sucked at his skin eagerly. Something slithered before him in the darkness, a tacky sound of moist flesh sliding against itself.

"Adrian! Is that you?"

His fingers brushed against the aluminum of the flashlight's handle. He wrenched it free of the fleshy mass that crept up the sides, pulling it in. He brandished it, standing, still trying to free his feet from the flesh that crawled up his jeans and slipped under the hem of his pants.

"Jaacob..." His flashlight's beam caught on the thing, and he nearly dropped the light again. The scream boiled out of his throat. "Jaaa... cob..." His brother's face hung before him, eyes glassy, protruding obscenely from a mass of flesh. The terribly canted joints of his fingers poked out of what might have once been his hand, and farther up the half-dissolved radius and ulna that must have once attached them to his body. The thing's mouth opened and closed, eyes pointing in different directions, eyelids draped unevenly.

"You... came..." The words tore from Adrian's mouth as if formed by something unfamiliar with human speech.

The organic matter of the walls seeped up along Jacob's legs, and a strange burning drew his attention to his toes. He struggled to free his feet, but was stuck fast. Adrian, or the Adrian-thing, made a wet sort of retching noise. Some dark liquid dribbled from the corner of his cow like eye. The needy pressure in his head, the presence of his brother, struck him now as terrifically alien, long since devoid of the flashes of human emotion that had always punctuated it in the past.

The flesh crept up his back and slid under the hem of his shirt. His hands scrabbled behind him, trying to claw at the sensation that was creeping along his spine. He could get no purchase, though, and a stabbing pain in his lower back made his eyelids jerked wildly open. He sobbed, and half-intelligible pleas tumbled from his lips.

More stabbing pain. Tearing. His blood ran messily, soaking into the waistband of his pants. The matter crept lovingly up his throat and plunged into his mouth, choking off his screams. The flesh hooked along his face and covered his eyes.

The puppet-like thing that had once been Adrian gurgled. "Welcome..."

SYMMETRY

I'd been fishing around in the closet for our luggage, but I extricated myself to look at her in disbelief.

"How could a system appear in empty space?"

In my haste, I knocked the basket of gloves on the floor and cursed. She laughed and bent down to help me pick them up.

"Gravitational lensing is our best guess," she said. "The system didn't just appear out of nowhere. Most of the information we get about distant systems is via EM radiation. Light. Gravity bends light like a lens which can lead to some strange results on telescopes. There's no reason that the same effect couldn't be used to bend the light from a specific place in space entirely away from us, so we'd only see blankness."

"Used?" I looked at her in time to catch her smile, pleased that I'd caught the important subtext.

I ran through the rote steps of preparation for deployment while we spoke: pinging HiveSpace to care for our cats, making sure the food plants were on auto-water and had a full tank, setting up my standard deployment greeting so that anyone who pinged me would know I was out in the stars somewhere.

"It wouldn't have to be a conscious agent making it happen, but it would be quite a surprise to discover that this sort of thing had happened by accident, especially given that light travels straight towards us from the system at a constant speed. In the cosmic scheme of things, we've only had the tech to travel to such a distant world for a few seconds. It's not impossible, but the likelihood dwindles to the point where another thinking being becomes a more appealing scenario, even to Occam, I should think."

I dialed the settings into the auto waterer as she spoke. This whole domestic scene, us preparing to leave; it was the sort of thing we'd lived over and over on mission after mission, subconscious in its familiarity.

But some detail of that familiarity had shifted, something about the way the midday light slanted through the blinds and sliced the snoozing cats into lazy bars of light and shadow and the smell of the coffee on the stove. I stared out through the half-drawn blinds, out at the looping plastisteel garden helices winding between the apartment towers, where drones pulled themselves along with long arms and drove spikes with machine precision into the green apostrophes of weed sprouts. The city had drawn the sunshade and the bright points of our sister-stars blew glimmering sparkles along its rippling length. A homesickness, perhaps, and we hadn't even left home yet.

Long ago, my ancestors had sailed the largest ocean of old Earth and peopled some of the most remote and beautiful places, dots of vibrant earth peeking out from an incomprehensibly vast ocean. Others came later with steel and steam, but my ancestors had been first, and they'd used their knowledge of the subtle interplay of wind, waves, and animal to carry them safely across the bosom of the world. Space was as much a part of me as the ocean had been a part of them, and I didn't know what to make of these new feelings.

"Is this something we have the tech to do? This gravity lensing?" I asked.

"Not in the slightest."

"Should I be concerned about this?"

"Concerned about the tech itself or concerned about SGS acquiring it?" she asked.

I shrugged. "Either."

"Yes, to both."

And if she was concerned, I sure was, too. As Chief Physics Researcher, Heke knew what she was talking about, especially with her focus on relativistic effects. "If you're worried, why are you going?" I asked. I was going because I was one of the top biologists at SGS for life definition work, but in all honesty, I'd already begun the process of abdicating my post, doing my best to train others to meet and surpass the knowledge I had. I wasn't on any real retirement track, not yet, but I flirted with the idea.

"I don't trust them," she said.

Heke had told me years before that she'd gotten her chromosomes stripped from their spermatic vessels and implanted into eggs once she heard I was interested in kids. We'd never really made plans anywhere but the middle-distant future about the whole thing, but that unfinished idea crossed my mind now, and like a ratcheting-forward, something static about me had become mutable. I could have had my own sperm frozen and at any time we could have had the geneminders combine our gametes into a blastula and halt it at that early stage. Not that it would make a difference if we both died on the mission, of course, but there was something comforting in the idea.

Heke was packing clothes when I wrapped myself around her from behind. "Let's go down to the canals for dinner tonight," I said, blowing the hair from her ear and kissing her on the lobe.

She did not turn to me, nor did she stop packing, but she relaxed into me and she felt like home. "Not in a rush to leave for once?" she said, her voice deadpan, but from long familiarity I knew she was teasing.

I had long since given up understanding how she could read my feelings when they seemed a muddle to me in the midst of them. "My treat."

The terminal was crowded when we arrived, but we flashed SGS badges and breezed past the mass of crying kids and pissed off parents waiting for body composition scans. The frustration on parents' faces was unmistakable, but I thought there might be some deeper peace under there. Some purpose. "Looks exhausting," said Heke. I flashed hot with weird resentment and turned myself away and towards the military boarding.

The day was cool and overcast with the suns' light beaming yellow-white through a scrim of turquoise methane clouds high in the atmosphere. We endured the resentful stares of waiting public passengers as we slipped to the front of the line, waved through by the SGS inspectors who pulled up our last recorded bodycomp scannings. The atmosphere was one of tired repetition, or perhaps that was just the creakiness in my joints as I settled myself into a too-small waiting chair for the umpteenth time as a concierge grabbed our luggage, imprinted them with a flashbadge, and shuttled them off to be loaded into the transport clipper.

Heke reclined in the chair next to me as I listened to the overhead announcements requesting passengers consume all food prior to bodycomp so as to keep the mass funneling process accurate, an announcement in galactic standard first of all and then repeated on a loop in ten or twelve SGS-recognized languages. I'd heard the damned thing so many times that I could even repeat the pattern of Czlithid clicks and screeches. She sighed and tapped away at something on her inlay, enfolding the holo display and working only in 2D. Then she shifted off of me, folding herself such that I wouldn't be able to see the screen, and jealousy flickered in my heart.

The same feeling gnawed at me watching her with her colleagues, sometimes, with whom she shared such a fluid, intellectual rapport. She told me in no uncertain terms that she would not cheat on me because there was no point; if there was someone else she wanted, she would leave me, and I believed her. She was no nonsense like that, and though it still baffled me why she'd want to be with a biologist instead of someone who could keep up with her in advanced math, she always laughed when I pointed this out.

"Love isn't about academic compatibility," she always said. "I get that from my coworkers. I get something else from you."

"What?" I would ask.

But she would only smile.

I am not proud to admit that infidelity was my first thought, coming so soon on the heels of the jealous rage that turned in my gut towards the families waiting in the pubterm, the complexity of my feelings towards her disinterested response to them. The jealousy rose, not from a fear of her disrespecting our relationship, but rather taking the form of a future denied, an interloper arriving to steal my wife from me before we had a chance to set her eggs to divide. Jealousy, and a sick upwelling of shame, for who was I to consider her or her gametes my property? I was glad she was distracted by her inlay because she could always read my face like a book.

In the SGS terminal, we were separated from the public by a bank of tinted glass and fake landcoral blooming with plastex polyps that waved in a way that seemed almost natural, as long as you didn't look long enough to figure out that their motion was repetitive. The sound of the crowds drifted over the top of the barrier, and my brain filtered out everything but the overlapping hums of travel HomeBots soothing babies, the laughing of kids, the pleased, tired murmurs of familial closeness. I reached out a hand and placed it on Heke's ankle and rubbed it gently, and she pushed her foot towards me without returning my look.

I got up to use the bathroom, resolving not to look at her inlay while passing behind her and failing utterly. What did I expect to see? Some evidence of infidelity, of a secret lover sending her missives that weren't intended for my eyes? What I saw instead was a message without a sender. My traitor eyes slowed my feet enough to let me read.

"if you meet the buddha, kill the buddha."

With relief bubbling up, tinged with shame, I could have laughed. "Is that a koan?" I asked.

She turned to me with a flat expression, the kind I associated with her neutral, computing mindset. "I guess so," she said.

The terminal display blinked and changed color to announce that dropship boarding would begin shortly.

The bridge had no windows, but the planetary surface on the display before us surged with varied topography and markers of life. An old Earth cousin with a surface half-splattered with the unmistakable shifting blueish of liquid water and crenelated with landforms as varied as any world I'd seen. Rusty red deserts with scalloped dunes, a circumpolar mountain range dotted with the albedo-white of ice, patchwork terrain in many colors but most especially a purple so dark as to be nearly black. I'd seen plenty of planets and no small number that were Earthlike, but this was by far one of the most captivating for its sheer variety. It could have been something an artist had rendered for a SGS recruitment ad, something to make a possible young recruit dream of the beauty of unseen worlds.

Heke and I stood on the bridge as the heads of Physics and Bio, with a handful of others from the planetary team leadership. I'd worked with some of them on previous missions— there was a tech I remembered had a wicked sense of humor and a couple of grad students who'd since graduated and were working on post-doc appointments in sentience physics and in geobio—but I didn't know anyone else by name, save for the Captain.

Captain Birungi looked tired; or maybe I was just projecting. We'd worked together plenty of times, especially in the last five or six standard years; SGS tended to keep functional teams together, since interstellar travel wasn't something where you wanted to risk personality differences derailing team effectiveness and safety. His dark brown skin showed a lifetime's worth of wrinkles that belied his age, somewhere in his early 50s, minus hyperlight travel time.

"There's a complication," he said, looking at the tech guy who stood next to him, a skinny, pale kid with red hair obviously genefactured in its cherry color. "Show them."

The kid nodded and tapped something on his inlay, and the display changed to a standard message log.

"An SOS," said the captain. "Galactic standard, and standard contents as well. Like something out of a military training holo, save for this last bit." The tech did something, and part of the message decrypted.

"When the many are reduced to one, to what is the one reduced?"

I started. I remembered the message Heke had been reading, the koan. I glanced at her as surreptitiously as I could, but she didn't react in any way, which was in and of itself weird. This was something she'd normally be curious about, I thought. My guts squirmed, and I tried to ignore it.

The captain continued, "As far as we can tell, it started broadcasting shortly after we jumped into the system, once we were a handful of light minutes away."

"No other information?" asked Heke.

"None," he said.

"We'll be responding to it," said a woman to my right in SGS fatigues. She had the drawn expression I associated with longtime military service, and her dark, curly hair was shorn nearly to her scalp. There was an edge of defiance in her tone that I read as defection to duty, and I took an immediate dislike to her.

"Of course, sergeant," said the captain. "But it's suspect, regardless. They started transmitting before the gravity waves from our arrival in-system could have reached the broadcast location, as if they knew we were coming."

"Could they have been transmitting before we arrived?" I asked.

He shrugged. "Possibly, but the signal is directionally boosted and points straight at our arrival vector."

There was a beat of silence as we processed this. Personally, I had no idea what to think. Physics had never been my strong suit, so I had to take them all at their word that this was weird. I asked the question that I think was on all of our minds: "How dangerous is this mission?"

The captain shook his head. "We don't know, but everything we've already seen, the appearance of the planet in the first place and now this, points towards some tech beyond what we currently have the ability to explain. We're proceeding with an assessment of maximum risk presently. So that means full kit for your squad, Sergeant."

The woman to my side, the angry-faced sergeant, nodded.

"And this means we'll be proceeding slowly, so inform your research teams this might not be like other canvassing missions. Speak to the quartermaster and make sure everyone is armed with at least a lightgun, and if anyone has experience with heavier projectile or plasma weapons, I'd like people kitted in whatever they are comfortable handling. We'll be dropping at 1600 hours standard."

...

"I still don't understand how it could have moved so fast," I said, slipping into the sleeping bag and watching Heke through sleep-blurry eyes as she undressed and put her hairpins on the folding table in our tent. The long, smooth lines of her melted seamlessly into the soft, organic shadows of the tent fabric, of the bundled blankets.

"Neither do we," she said, "but it's in keeping with what we've already seen with respect to hyperlight functionality. If we assume that there's something here that can exceed the speed of light, it would be perfectly possible that the signal blinked away from us."

"That seems like a big assumption," I said.

"It is, but it's what we're working with."

The night proved to be a warm one. We'd landed as close to the signal as we could, in a wide, clear plain that proved perfect for touchdown with plenty of clear surface area. Almost suspiciously perfect, and as if to confirm the strangeness, the SOS signal had flickered to the west a couple hundred klicks, into the heart of what looked like a jungle. Some of the meteorology researchers were debating whether some kind of atmospheric effect could have distorted the message direction before we'd cleared the ionosphere, but for the most part, they'd accepted the readings as a reality we would now be forced to contend with.

Worse yet, we were working on the limited energy resources of an early exploration crew. We could make a couple trips with the drop ship to and from the surface of the planet, but we couldn't afford to battle the atmosphere over and over. We had to pick a spot and then be prepared to travel on foot or risk getting stranded, so we'd pitched camp and the ground team had, with the input of the nav/mapper team on the orbital ship, charted our journey westward.

The camp we'd established was a cozy one, the tents looking anachronistic and fragile despite their ability to weather even a substantial gas-giant storm. We'd landed in a field of blue-green blades of grass, as wide as a finger and as long as a forearm. The grass edges were sharp enough to give you a nasty slice if you caught them the wrong way, but we'd set down some mats beneath the tents. And camping on the edge of that great field, with waves of blue on one side and a forest of round, dark trees on the other, gave the impression of camping on the edge of a vast ocean.

Enkidu, the name the geobiologists had coined since the SGS designator MX00022.35//24 was a mouthful, was Earthlike-enough to be comfortable without envirogear but just different enough to be obvious. The gravity was 1.1 that of Earth's, leading to a slight feeling of lethargy all the time, fighting the extra force.

Something about the atmosphere lent itself to forming the most beautiful sunsets I had ever seen: neon pink and orange and lime green and even patches of lavender, all mixing with feathered edges around the clouds of thin, wispy ice flakes high in the atmosphere. The mycocanvas of the shelter fluttered above us, giving every impression of lightness. I thought I could die happy in that moment there with her, with or without kids.

"The biophysicists are like little kids at rev-end," she said as she slipped into the sleeping bag with me, nestling her slight form around the outside of my larger one, resting her chin on my upper back. "Someone detected some weird gravitational behavior and someone else has already been running micro spectroscopic collections, like peeking into presents before it's time to open them. It's a goldmine already. Point nine six Earthlike, and there's already fascinating things in the microbes."

"To say nothing of this mysterious, faster-than-light tech."

"Quite." She shifted. "One of my students was talking about silicon-based organic molecules."

I felt myself bristle. "Might as well leave that. It's outside Params. Personal curiosity can come later, after we've done what we came here to do."

"Personal curiosity," she said, as if she were tasting the phrase.

My shoulders tensed up, despite trying not to. "I don't make the Params," I said, my face reddening with the defensiveness.

"But you enforce them."

A statement, not a question. She would leave it there, and so would I. We'd had too many fights about my job, and I had no energy to continue today. How could I admit that she might be right, and that the fact that she was right made me want to settle down and stop all this and start a new life, a family life, when she hadn't come to the same conclusion?

We had worked alongside one another for almost twenty years, more if you counted those long, forgotten years in the deep freeze spinning our way towards different worlds. I had warned her that I would never want to settle and that being with me would be tantamount to perpetual military spouse syndrome. If she was going to find herself baby crazy in a couple of years and looking for a house on Arcturus or one of the nebular colonies then she'd be better off saddling up with someone else. She'd just smiled her knowing smile at me.

We'd fallen in love on missions much like this, us bonding over the overlap between our fields and the strange, alien beauty of the planets we visited, new worlds that we evaluated for human habitation, thrilling in the fascinating ways in which chemistry blossomed into the macro and brought about shapes and forms of movement and beauty never seen before. And, in many cases, never seen since.

Most planets we had been to had been one-time trips; we came, we evaluated against the Params, and then once we checked the "no sentient life" box, after us came the colonization teams and their scouring beams and terraformers. Turning these worlds of strange, unique beauty into something as Earthlike as could be managed. I hadn't given this much thought myself, my face always turned towards the next new, strange world, but I thought it wore on Heke. And when things wore on her, they came to wear on me as well.

This idea hadn't bothered me in the beginning. There were simply so many worlds out in space, and the work we were doing meant very little in the grand scheme of things when there were countless exoplanets in our galaxy, to say nothing of the larger universe. Some people called it Earth-Orphan thinking, the reductiveness in those of us with strong ties to a planet thoroughly destroyed that led to us thinking of other planets as similarly destructible. But perhaps after enough time, the deaths of all those worlds did begin to wear on me, whether or not I ever saw them again.

I sighed, a sound of surrender. Heke didn't look at me, but her hand drifted to my collarbones and rested on the flat of my chest. I fell asleep not long afterwards.

...

Despite its beauty, moving across Enkidu was heavy jungle trekking. With all the uncertainty, we were in full kit with our hapt suits. Our lightguns would have made short work of the twining vines, but there were just so damn many of them and we didn't want to burn the place down, so we mostly used sonic knives. I would have credited SGS with some notion of ecology had I not known that they would have readily torched the whole damn planet if it wasn't so costly to rebuild a shattered biosphere.

After the signal had flicked away from us, it held its position, about 200 klicks to the west into the heart of the jungle. We had a single four-wheeler for our gear, and we were on foot.

Despite the hapt suit's built-in air conditioning, I dripped with sweat. We'd reached the edge of a ridge in the forest that we had been following in a quest for some height. We had our nav team on the ship guiding us, but when you're boots on the ground, a little height is never something to complain about. It was just nearing average solar midday. The light of the two suns merged into a red-gold burst, the red giant currently nearer and occluding much of the younger star that was its pair in the binary. The sunlight dripped from the round, purple-black leaves of the trees we'd stared calling cabbage heads, carried to the floor on the nutrient-rich gel that dripped from the underside of the leaves, glistening like honey in the sunset. A desire for banana pancakes and syrup washed through me, and a homesickness for our apartment on Hydraxis and sleepy Saturdays spent with a brunch picnic by the canal.

Enkidu spread before us as a lush rainforest, resplendent in deep oranges and purples. Some stands were pure black, a devouring visual darkness that one of the bio guys had explained allowed them to absorb even more wavelengths of sunlight. It had the effect of making it seem like certain parts of the forest were cast into inexplicably deep shadow, or perhaps were just missing altogether. I'd heard one of them talking about carbon fibers in the hushed tones of young romance.

We were caught up in the view, so it shocked me out of my reverie when one of the ground patrol guys yelled "contact!" and I heard the clack of pulse rifles lifted to eyes and primed.

"Hold!" called Sergeant Mxo.

I followed their barrels to the disturbance. A soft, white-brownish hexapodal entity stood to the west along the ridge. Its skin glistened damply. The top of its body collected water in big beads. The underside fluttered with thin gills, like a mushroom. I lifted my tablet and started recording as fast as I could, almost dropping the device in the process.

"If it approaches within twenty yards, take the shot, but leave it otherwise," said the sergeant.

But it did not approach. We hadn't seen where it had come from, but clots of rusty-red dirt covered it, like the dirt underneath our feet, and it plodded silently along until it reached the base of one of the cabbage heads. I realized that the mass of detritus under the tree was not simply roots and other plants, but that something had died there.

"Can I get closer?" I asked. "I want to see what that is."

"No," said the sergeant. "Use your scope. We don't want to take any risks."

Through the scope, I saw not just one but several small, dead bodies, small mammals, or something mammal-like. This world's homologue to the rodents of old Earth, perhaps, something which always seemed to show up in a food web dominated by movement-evolved beings. We'd missed them because their fur blended in so well with the spray of grassy plant life beneath the trees, but now looking for them I turned my scope elsewhere and, to my surprise, I realized this was not the only pile of tiny corpses beneath a cabbage head.

We'd seen critters licking the sap from the leaves of the tree; could they have been caught there in a trap? Perhaps poisoned? I made a note to take a sample and see what we could discern.

Meanwhile, the hexapodal mushroom thing had reached the pile, and it moved itself to straddle the matter below with its six legs.

"What's it doing?" asked one of the interns next to me.

"Shh," I said. "Just watch."

There was a disgusting, wet slapping noise as the thing disgorged something from its underside. It looked white and sticky and immediately made me think of a net of mycelium.

"What the hell?" called the sergeant.

"I think it's eating," I said.

And, indeed, the net that it had exuded had pulsed and grown and spread over the pile until it covered the whole of it. The creature itself was silent, but I imagined all the slides I'd seen in grad school of hyphae working their way between cells, expressing their digestive juices and siphoning up nutrients. "I'd love to get some samples of this. It looks like an external stomach. Maybe some kind of mobile saprophyte. Very cool."

"Sentient, you think?" joked one of the interns.

"There's no indication of anything to make us believe we're looking at sentience," I said, with more harshness than I meant. Heke gave me a hard look, but I ignored it.

"Looks like it's busy with its meal," said the sergeant. "Protocol says we should move on, but if we find another one of those piles, maybe with the external stomach left on, you can take your sample."

I woke to the light from her inlay even though it was set on low-light redshift night settings, and I tried not to show that she'd woken me. Normally, I slept deeply, but my body had been on the fritz the entire trip. Nothing was settling right for me.

I want to be clear, whatever you think of me as a partner, that I did not previously make a habit of looking at what she did on her own devices. That was none of my business unless she wanted to show me. But worry gnawed at me, and I looked.

The tent canvas snapped around us in irregular concert and wind hissed against the fabric. We'd camped on the edge of a river that channeled the night wind. We were still a few days from the beacon location and there were a lot of jokes about what we'd do if it moved again, but we were content. There was just so much to explore. After a couple days of startling encounters with fauna that seemed entirely disinterested in our presence, the ground team had let us put down a more substantial base camp in the evening. The bio cohort had been busy all evening taking samples of the purple-ish water, the red soil, scrapings from cabbage heads, samples of the leavings of the mushroom creatures.

I'd hung around for a bit, but secretly I'd been thankful that my role was one of oversight rather than research. Watching the post docs compare known organic molecular bond-angles to what they saw in some of these new, novel structures, many of which included both carbon and silicon in their structures and making all those red Xs: novel molecule, inorganic, no evidence for life, for sentience. It broke my heart.

Heke would have been proud, I imagined, if I'd had the heart to tell her, but she'd been distant all evening, barely picking at her dinner and then retiring so early to the tent. She'd been wrapped up in her inlay more and more. She'd always been the type to excuse herself from social interactions to read papers, but this was furtive, secret, entirely unlike her, and it made me nervous.

So no, I wasn't proud, but I was concerned. And we often justify the way we hurt others as concern for them, don't we?

On her screen was a conversation window. Again, no name, but a long message:

"Bodhidharma sat in a cave for nine years gazing at the wall. Hui-ke arrived to inquire about the dharma, but Bodhidharma refused to teach him. Finally, taking a knife, Hui-ke cut off his own arm and presented it as an offering to Bodhidharma, who agreed to become his teacher."

Her fingers hovered over the keyboard as if she was attempting to come up with a reply.

I almost moved, almost said something, almost forgot that I was supposed to be asleep. It was another koan, of course; I'd heard this one before, or some variation of it. But it seemed somehow threatening.

She hadn't said a word to me about this. There had been an opportunity to do so at the shuttle terminal, but we'd been moved along and I'd forgotten, and she'd never brought it back up. She was the kind of partner who didn't forget things like that; she

often continued conversations I'd forgotten we'd been having earlier.

Did she ever have to pause like this when she talked to me? Did she ever not immediately have a response? Did I ever put her off-balance like this, engage the whole of that brain of hers?

I turned over roughly and made a noise like I was still asleep. Shortly thereafter, the light from her inlay winked off.

Feng clapped a hand onto my shoulder. "Nice try, dude, you're not getting away this time!"

I held up my hands and laughed. "Fine, fine." I played it off like nothing was wrong, like I hadn't actually been avoiding them. "What've you got for me?"

"Amazing, amazing stuff with these samples." They pulled up some molecular visualizations on their inlay. "Totally weird, not even close to earthlike save for the necessary molecular geometries. But really, really novel stuff."

The ground team ordered the packed camp structures piled into the transport and did their best to urge the science teams into action, but my team, in particular, moved slow. Multiple of them had requested I ask to post up for another couple days to do some more detailed studies, and I'd had to remind them that we listened to the ground team first and foremost and that an SOS took priority over research, and that, if the SOS was the result of some hitherto unforeseen danger, we'd best be listening to the people with the guns who could protect us if something on this planet turned out to be human-aggressive.

The morning was coming on hot, another cloudless day where the shade from the trees would keep us cool and the sun would sweat us. Heke appeared from the mouth of the tent, pale and ragged. She drank mug after mug of tea and said nothing to me, and suspicion chewed holes in my stomach that I did my best to ignore.

Feng flicked through a list of the polymers they'd discovered thus far, waxing poetic about lattice structures and diffusion coefficients, and I nodded along, my dread pushing uncomfortably against the edges of my forced smile. Even when they weren't trying to, they classified everything as it related to our mission, the mission of the SGS, and in deference to the Params, that single, rigid description of "life" as "Earthlike life" that allowed us to so neatly remove from our bubble of consideration those organisms that lived with different electron transport chains, with biochemistry of their own.

This had never bothered me before; after all, I was an expert on Earthlike life and deeply passionate about the magic of our particular form of energy transfer, but I'd seen too much to think there was anything special about it, now.

And had Heke always known this? I could see, now, how I'd been something of a bigot, a lover of the things that were familiar, and while I would not have thought of myself as excluding these other forms of chemistry, by promoting my own biology I had demoted others.

Feng looked at me with an expectant smile. I'd totally lost the train of their explanation.

I smiled, and put a hand on their shoulder. "Very cool stuff," I said, and turned to walk off, trying to hide my embarrassment.

...

The ravine took us by surprise even though we were expecting it from the ship's terrain mappings. Full dark had fallen, but the sky to the east still glowed cherry-red with the afterimage of the departed second sun. The orientation of sun to ravine left the glow at what appeared to be the termination of the ravine on our visual horizon, making it seem like the sun set into the crack. Its dying light painted the walls of the cliff with blood.

The edges of the ravine were ragged, but smoothed enough by the passage of time to communicate that the planetary wound was not fresh. Cabbage heads still grew nearly to the edge of it, and the roots dangled into empty space, trailing unexpected globes of bioluminescence within them that dotted their length for tens or even hundreds of meters into the ravine.

I sidled up to Feng, whose eyes were fixed in rapt concentration on their tablet.

"What's up?" I asked. "You've got a look in your eye."

I'd kept myself out of the loop; there had been a lot of excited chatter about the cabbage heads, but I'd passed over it as best as I could, not really wanting to know anything about a new, interesting organism that would soon be scoured off the face of the planet and replaced with yogurt shops. But now I found my scientific curiosity overwhelmed my denial, and I needed to know what I was seeing.

"The network," they breathed, pinching and zooming out. "We've been trying to use our limited geoscan options to map this; the roots of the things seem way more convoluted than we'd expect. At first, we were trying to figure out if it was a complex structural anchoring mechanism; the soil here is fairly sandy and the trees are tall, so we thought it could be somehow keeping them upright, but the scanning we've done so far showed them going deeper and interconnecting in ways that exceed what would be necessary for structural support. But this ravine is perfect; I've got the drone up." They nodded towards the ravine, and I could see the little thing buzzing away, scanning along the exposed face in neat rows, and the data loaded into Feng's screen, filling a map of what appeared to be the root connections.

"What's that gradient?" I asked, pointing to the colors along the map.

"This is going to fuck you up," they said, "pardon the language. But they're electrical impulses."

"Steady ones?" I asked, feeling my heart sink, realizing it would have leapt a few years prior when I was still excited about this work, hoping I was misunderstanding.

"No, that's just the static scan state of the system. Here, let me pause it and show a real-time display."

I almost asked them not to; it might've been preferable to just not know what would be lost. Nothing to mourn that way.

The screen thought for a moment, and then loaded a local slice of the network, but pulsing with life. And not just life, but signals. I'd spent enough time working on sentience to have strong feelings on this issue. One of the ways we distinguished sentience from random patterns of activity was a purposeful patterning. A sense of randomness, but the organized randomness of life, of intelligence. Natural phenomena not driven by sentience tended to produce patterns that were at once simple and complex and rarely anywhere in the middle; either the complete randomness of pure noise and static, like the measurements of the average height of the ocean at a specific GPS location over time, or simple order, like the periodicity of day/night cycles on planets orbiting a single star.

"Don't worry, I've already started measuring against Param standards. Yes, it's looking complex, but so far there's not more than a kilobyte of actual information stored per minute or so of scan time. Obviously, we'll need to do more collection, but we're looking at low-grade random-class phenomena here. Nothing to be concerned about."

"Glad to hear it," I said. I swallowed. "And this... network effect, this spreads throughout the planet?"

"Everywhere the trees are, at least, we think," they said. "Kind of cool. If it was sentience, we'd be looking at a conscious forest. Maybe a conscious planet." They looked around. "But like I said, no one's talking about anything like that."

Heke looked at me pointedly, and I turned away.

Evenings on Enkidu wore thin to the dusky warmth of night, with its jeweled beetles in flight, the shards of sunset glinting off their carapaces. Heke looked thinner and thinner each day. She had always trended to the sturdier, in muscle and in fat, and the weight loss wore her like a mannequin. Her fire remained, though. It was not that she wasted away, but rather that she burned herself to the end of the wick.

The signal disappeared, of course, soon after we'd reached the ravine.

We waited as the ground team decided what we'd do next, but my brain had gone blank, had melted into the sunsets that burned like the end of the world.

On so many mornings, her tired smiles glowed in the strange, dark pastel blue of the first predawn, picked out in threads of joy, in sparks of laughter, in a flurry of the soft wings of the moth-like things that bumped against the tents at night, seeking the light. The day would crack before me like a golden yolk, running down towards some strange distances that I could not know if we might return from.

One of the big, many-winged bird things made its way out of the distant forest that ringed the grasslands, lumbering slowly into the air. We lay in our tent; the sun fading fast, the sides open to the breath of the strange world around us. I lay there, smelling the soft, cottony scent of her hair spread on the pillow beside me, brain awash and empty.

"They ruled on Alpha Praetor," she said. "Full scouring and rebuild."

I rubbed my face, trying to remember. "Was that... hydrogen sulfide?"

She nodded. "They invoked the oxygen reduction Param. The planet is so Earthlike that the requisite terraforming won't be much beyond provoking some simple geological processes and the thing should be humming along and ready for seedships in a matter of decades."

We lay in silence for a moment, and I remembered Alpha Praetor, the startling red of the sunsets and the way the crimson sky spun with long, thin banners like cursive stretched across horizons. "It's ribbons," I said, remembering. "Ribbons of silicone blowing through the upper atmosphere like flags." And I wondered what it would be like to be a living, dreaming part of the sunset.

"It's empire," she said. "That's all. They're trying to justify it with science. They used to use race, and then freedom. And now they're using science."

I had nothing I could say to that.

In time, Heke moved against me, and in time, we moved together, and there was sweetness and surrender in it, and a terrible, beautiful sense of finality.

"Would you use the eggs?" she asked, afterwards.

Lying there in the tent, my arm folded between us, nestled in the warm hollows of her back, the ending lay heavy on my heart. But the moment was one not of loss but of transformation. I knew she had always been borrowed, not owned, and that she would leave my life as unexpectedly as she had entered it.

"Yes," I said.

A relaxing, then. And soon, her breath slid into easy sleep, a rare thing for her.

In the months after our return from Enkidu they'd talked about it with me over coffee dozens of times.

Each time, they assured me it wasn't an interrogation and interrogated me anyway, them in their SGS-standard fatigues and their hard, practiced smiles and their conversational scripts that I recognized bits and pieces from. Ways to get answers without seeming like you were seeking them. Ways to probe for loyalty, for secrets.

They called it Kanon. They couldn't tell me anything more about it, about what it had been, or who, or where. They just had the record of messages exchanged, koans and equations, philosophy and science.

I had nothing I could offer them. They knew more than I. Their messages told the whole of the story I had only caught in glimpses. According to what they found when they cracked her inlay (and, of course, they didn't say they cracked it, but of course she hadn't just left it un-encrypted), she had been talking to Kanon for months prior to the deployment, prior to the appearance of Enkidu, even, and while it seemed only to speak in Buddhist riddles and in equations I hardly understood beyond knowing they had something to do with relativity, I understood well enough that she had been courted by this Kanon.

I could have laughed that there were still some flickers of jealousy in the periphery of my limbic system, even after everything that had happened, as if this Kanon had been a secret lover and not...

Well, that bit comes next.

By morning, she had gone.

She had not stirred me with her leaving, and I thought this just as well. Had I wakened, I might have tried to stop her even though I knew I could not have.

I took the gravlift up the ravine face to the plateau above. Deep, purplish clouds worried the distant horizon, but the sky above me spread pink and orange. My heart wanted space to fix the memories of this strange and beautiful world alongside my final memories of my wife, before the rest of the camp awoke and discovered what had happened.

And she would not leave forever without saying goodbye.

The sound presaged its appearance, a metallic chittering like a knife chipping shards of ice. I turned towards the east, the compass of my heart tugging me into final alignment with what was to come.

It stood before me, steel thorns glimmering blade-edged in the exultant dawn light that burst upon us, all carmine and golden. My eyes struggled to resolve its form; the impossible brightness of the sun poured between knives that curved inwards like a ribcage, and I shielded my eyes from the glare. Great, arched legs of blades suspended the shape above the ground, and I wondered how it didn't sink into the soil on their needle-thin points. My brain could not determine if it was human-sized and near enough to touch or massive and distant, its spider-like limbs wrapping the planet in a steel embrace. My heart pulsed with soft vulnerability, standing there with those razor-edged limbs arcing above me, spanning all the sky.

"Take them and go." The voice was Heke's, stretched and quantized and underwritten with countless others. My hand found my gun, though it seemed only drawn there by a magnetism of its own. There was something of the profane in the concept of using it, my body curiously stilled even in its presence. Perhaps it was the certainty of death, the way its gleaming steel arms had folded open as if ratcheting into place, though the mechanism was grace and silence, isotonic equilibrium. I thought of the planets, flung wide in ever-decaying orbits, the stars devouring themselves, the deep time in which all information decays, and thought it might still hold the force at bay that vectored towards me from the leading edges of those blades. A derivative of infinity, a surrender.

"Take them and go."

The words washed over me like static, my brain slow to absorb their meaning. My eyes adjusted to the blinding light. My heart sought the form of my wife within the shifting metallic heart. The facets of faces, Heke's narrowed eyes, the set of her lip when she was determined; they skittered and rippled across the chromed uncertainty of its form.

My eyes strained to shift focus to parts of its being which flickered, impossibly distant, then near enough to touch. My heart glittered with awe, with all of the love I'd ever held for her blasting through me all at once and streaming down my face in joyful tears.

"Where are you?" I asked her.

There were some crackling voices heard upside-down or backwards. The sounds of lush jungle morning fading shudderingly into a diffraction pattern of static. The thready, phantom doubling, trebling of birdsong, artifacted and warmed.

Her laughter, a recording or a memory. "Delocalized in spacetime." The laugh again. "It's okay."

"You're okay?" I raised my hand towards her, the warmth of the dawn cast from her blades like heartbreak, my skin glowing amber and burgundy. I ached to feel the molecular perfection of her bleeding edge, now. To feel her, not just pressed against the borders of me, but between, among, mingled with the stuff of me.

"We're not staying here. They won't be able to follow us. Take them and go."

A fist of pain clenched in my chest. She was going, now, like I had always known she would. Fear melted me to my knees, flowing into the red soil below.

"Is this what you want?"

For a moment, my own bloody ruin reflected in the springing tension of her beautiful scalpels, nicking the very edge of things, the dawn bleeding its glut of crimson. Then, the image blinked with parallax, and the distance between my skin and her edges resolved, further than the bulging, bright disks of galaxies throwing their arms of worlds before them into the darkness.

"There's so much to learn," she said.

There was sound to the west of me: the gravlift, shouts, the readying of rifles. Sounds from another life. In the gleaming chrome minarets of her mind and form, such sounds carried little significance, and I did not pay them much mind. My heart, my being, was too full of her dawn-blushing edges.

"Doc!" someone shouted.

"Hold!" I shouted.

Her shape twisted and burned against my retinas. Her smile was a flicker of signal in an ocean of noise, and when her blades retreated, they drew back across the world and through time, snicking back into their armed position. Their burning mercury lines carved the sky into non-Euclidean planes, symmetries warped and yet preserved, our paralleled lives intersecting again, but not now.

"We'll see each other again." Her voice dopplered, already stretching away from me, but the gleaming lines of her world-spanning arms danced with images of our reunion: a moment where she cleaved to the very heart of me, stilling my biochemical process but preserving the pattern of me in some deeper, stranger way. Some moment that was already occurring, had already occurred, would always be occurring. I rubbed my head.

In the space between blinks, she was gone, and all was silent. Then a spasm torqued my shoulders and back and I leaned over and barfed onto the rusty clay of the river basin.

"Doc!" Two simultaneous thuds as the medtech fell to her knees, pressing the sticky cool of a healthscan to my throat.

"I'm all right," I said, raising a hand to the scanner. My head throbbed. My heart sang in joyous exultation.

The sun's angle had deepened, bronzing the emerald of the slumbering jungle. I sank into rapturous peace with the knowledge that my existence was book-ended so neatly by those silvered blades retracting with the calculus of impossibly smooth motion until symmetry collapsed them, inverting the forces and canceling one another out, the arcing beauty of her passing through the impossible, empty space that was the vastness of my atoms, a limit that approached zero. What was there to fear when the perturbation of my existence would meld, had melded, was forever melding with such brilliance?

CONJUGATION

His hair was dark, as were his eyes.

I watched him from above. The candlelight played delightfully with his high cheekbones, his sharp, narrow jaw. He cradled books under one arm with a forest-green coat draped over the other, his eyes distant as he waited in line and focused on some far-flung place beyond his glasses.

I had chosen my place of observation with care, a solitary nook in the lofted upper floor of the coffeehouse. The sound of the street outside—the shouting, the sounds of horseshoes on cobbles, the ringing of church bells—didn't make it much past the front door, but something about the architecture of the space cast a delicious quiet over the loft, and I craved the respite from the din of city life.

What little room there was in the loft existed between shelves crammed with volumes. I liked the space as much for its quiet as I did for the smell of all those yellowed pages pressing me between them. A rich scent, papery and floral, and as much the smell of those bindings and sheaves of paper as it was the smell of the oils from the skins of the countless readers who had turned their pages.

The winter daylight hung in the air around us, captured in the milky translucence of the diamond-paned windows. The sound of voices smoothed and rounded its glaring edges. The smell of espresso, of rich, smoked teas, offset its wintry coldness.

I had come to Perry's Coffee to work, as I often did. I had also come to hunt.

I sipped my espresso and observed my muse as he shuffled forward. There was a look of displacement about him, a man whose thoughts were elsewhere. His face bore a shadow of beard, his skin medium-brown and spotted with pale patches. He wore his hair in tousled locs, several of which spilled over his face, though he seemed not to notice. I wondered what sound he might make if I were to tangle my fingers in it and yank his head back to expose the tender skin of his throat.

I closed my eyes. Breathed in deep the smell of the books. Exhaled. My heartbeat thumped uncomfortably in my chest, my dead heart overworked. No, this would not do.

I opened my eyes. Sipped my espresso, focusing on the richness of the flavor—dark cherries, pomegranate, browned butter, and burned sugar. My muse had slipped out of sight, under the edge of the balcony, and something loosened slightly in me enough for my gaze to return to my work.

My notebook lay open before me; the spell caught mid-sentence, but the words sat lifeless on the page. A love spell, a spell to rekindle a romance between a dear friend and her distant husband, the sort of thing I would normally lose myself in with ease, but the blue of the ink, the purposeful slanting of my penmanship, it exerted no pull on me.

Certainly, I could imagine no small number of happy endings for them. A blizzard, no uncommon happening in December, might kick up and bury the doors of their manor house, keeping them trapped together with nothing but the fires in the fireplaces for company.

Vintages might be opened from the wine cellar, and Luis might remark that he had been saving them for a special occasion and Eloise would suggest that it might be a special occasion, their being trapped there until the stableboys could dig the carriage out again. Perhaps there was poetry in it.

They would dress in their formal finest, making light of it, but each of them feeling within a pull to earlier, simpler days, to the dinner parties and balls where they'd met and courted.

Eloise would do her makeup as she had done then, bolder and unafraid of the way the powder sat in the creases in her face. Luis would feel again a connection to that young man in his velvet dinner jacket, a young man full of hunger for the world and not yet mired in the fear that he had wasted his life.

They would smile upon seeing one another, laughing, but each finding an unexpected burning within them to see the other so bold, no longer youthful, but bearing their age about them as the honor it was and not the burden it had become.

If I were simply to write a pretty dream like this for Eloise, perhaps she would be comforted by the words, but they would do nothing beyond that. But she did not pay me to dream for her. The words of the spell remained dead on the page, but I did not worry them to action. The magic would come and the words would bubble from that deeper well in their own time. That was the nature of the Gift.

And how easy it would be to use the Gift to nudge my dark-eyed interest towards me with prose. The threads in my mind waved gently, encouraging me to grasp them. They tantalized with introductions: the tapping sound of his scuffed leather boots on the stairs as he made his way to the unoccupied table near me, the way he would settle in and try to neaten his messy hair, attention drawn to the texts in his satchel.

It took everything within me not to grab the threads and follow them to their conclusions. Though I might stop writing the spell at any time, I could not undo what I had already written. Whatever disturbance I made in the weft of the world would move forward of its own accord like a dropped stitch.

No, I would allow this thing to play out of its own accord. I was certainly not averse to using the Gift to bring prey to me, but tugging on the heart of my muse would destroy the romance of the thing.

I wondered to myself if this was courtship, and despite myself, I smiled.

An unwillingness to use the gift was not an unwillingness to tilt fate in my favor. I'd been coming to Perry's for weeks, perhaps months, to glimpse him. It was only a matter of time before an introduction became inevitable, and fate smiled on me on a chilly morning garlanded with pine boughs and candle stubs, mere days from the solstice.

As I waited for service, my muse entered the shop, the bell tinkling as if to draw my attention. His smell wafted toward me on the winter wind, iron-gall ink, tannins, and beeswax.

His eyes did not meet mine as he entered, absorbed as he was in a book. He loosened his scarf and unbuttoned his green wool coat and took his place behind me in line. The loosening of the scarf revealed enough of his skin for me to feel my own humors rise, the lighter patches like petals scattered across his throat.

"Pardon my intrusion, but what's that you're reading?"

He looked up with the irritation of a scholar distracted from his study. "Xavro's Verses," he said, returning his attention to the page. His rudeness interested me all the more, I must admit. I so enjoy a challenge.

"In the original Hvarian?" I asked, emboldened.

He glanced up with raised eyebrows. "You're familiar?"

"There are few alive today who could read this text, even with the help of a dictionary," I said. "I am not among them. I'm given to believe the honorific cases are terribly arcane, even to those of us familiar with other early Warring-era tongues. They reflect a society stratified in a wholly different way from ours, a military gentry rather than an aristocracy."

His eyes widened. "You seem to know a great deal about this," he said, his shoulders straightening. "You're correct; though languages as a rule tend to reflect and enforce the mores of the society they grow within, Hvarian is unique in that the constructs of the military are built into the cases and declensions, and any scholar who endeavors to read any Hvarian texts requires a thorough understanding of their military caste system to parse." His accent was faint, but I could hear the suggestion of trilled Rs and a musical lilt to the phonemes that made me guess his first language was La Spezian.

"Quite an effort to study such a complex language, given that Hvary was destroyed by the Gallics almost thirteen centuries ago." I smiled and held out my hand. "Dorian," I said. "Dorian Allwether."

"Giovanni Capo," he said, adjusting his glasses. He took my hand, and I shook it with pleasure.

"Do you teach at the school, Giovanni?"

He frowned. "I've been told once too often that I wear my profession on my sleeve." He fidgeted with his tie, though it remained loose around his throat. "Classics," he said. "Folklore, language, ritual."

"The relics of our forebears."

"Is that a polite way of saying 'dusty, antiquarian nonsense'?"

My smile widened. "I have a great respect for the past," I said. "Too frequently, we look to the future. We find ourselves hitched to dreams of what will be with no grounding in the present. We tilt towards an imagined future without any anchor to the past, and we fail to learn from our mistakes."

There was suspicion in his eyes, and I liked that. Too often, prey came to me with open arms. Let him be a challenge, then.

"You didn't answer my question," he said.

"I suppose it is a polite way of saying that, yes," I said. "But if I poke fun at you, I do so at my own peril. I find myself enchanted by these studies as well." The suspicion did not leave his eyes, but I thought I saw a softening there, and an opening. I slipped my hand into my waistcoat, pulled out my card, and pressed it into his hand. "I have business elsewhere today, but I hope you might come to call on me sometime, if you'd like to discuss more. It is so rare that one finds a scholar of these things. There are many questions I would like to ask you."

His expression remained neutral, but he slipped the card into the inner pocket of his tweed jacket rather than the outer where it might be lost, and the snare tightened.

You might wonder if, in those moments, guilt plagued me, because my interest in Giovanni was not solely as my prey. It was far too easy to feed on the unwilling, to treat humans as nothing more than vessels for blood, and I did this at times when my need was great. But there were many reasons I had left my family estate and made a pariah of myself, and this was one; I found the hunt too delightful to ignore.

All the aunts and uncles called it childish, foolish. "This is how we were caught, before," they had told me in my youth. "You would undo all the work of your forefathers." But one does not choose the art he is drawn to create in the world, and my art played out upon the canvas of the mortal mind.

That evening, I returned to my apartments in a state of dizzy joy. The bursting orange of the winter's sunset had gilded the southern reaches of clouds and cast their northern sides in dusky navy, scrolling strange figures in a sky while stars pricked into view. The moon hung just above the horizon, days from her fullness and silvery-fat in the crisp air.

The breeze from the street entered behind me and kicked up dust from the corners of the floor. I checked the mail slot and discovered a calling card; without unsealing it, I recognized the handwriting as Lord Forsythe's. I smiled to myself and left it there for later inspection. I kicked my snow-damp boots off by the door and stepped into my slippers.

Only embers remained in the fireplace, so I stoked it, my mind lost in the memory of Giovanni.

I wondered if he would call. I was certain he would, truly. No mortal had ever been able to resist me, not once I'd turned my full attention to them.

I yawned as I sat at my writing desk, still shaking off the sleep from my mind, but the words already began to pour from me in a hot fury. I did not stop to read what I wrote; I was in a sleep-haze, and more, I did not want to know. It was the Gift; it having manifested in my dreams and then peeled my eyes open just as the first suggestion of dawn made itself known behind the rooftops of the city.

That which I sold of my services represented but a fraction of the way the Gift made itself known to me. I sold pulp-tales that I could scribble off in a minute when the inspiration struck, but when the Gift bloomed in its fullness and showed me that the me I held dear was a tiny piece of what existed within me, those were the only times that fear truly raised its icy head.

When I wrote from this place, the words seemed to come through me rather than from me; something else drove the scratching of the nib across the parchment. I wrote under the light of a stub of guttering candle, the Gift not seeing fit for us to light the lamps, even, in its haste. Though I tried not to read what I wrote, I could not miss the words that my brain clung to: the name of my muse, words that suggested hunger, passion, power, lust.

I thought, as I often did, that I was not in possession of my hands, and so I could not be held accountable for Giovanni's fate.

104

I stuffed the crumbled parchment into the embers of the stove. Certain turns of phrase sparkled through my brain, but not enough to reveal to me the story as it was to unfold. I feared to know what I had set in motion, what had been set in motion through me.

The man who opened the door was stocky and olive-skinned, and his mustaches had been waxed with care. "Afternoon," he said, waving me in. "I've got an appointment in an hour, but if you're looking for something quick, a shave, a tooth extraction, I can fit you in now."

I took off my hat and smiled. "No, sir, thank you. You must be Matteo. I'm here for Giovanni. Dorian Allwether." I held out a hand.

A dark crease formed between his eyebrows, but he took my hand with a grip that showcased all the strength of his muscle-banded forearms beneath the cuffed sleeves of his shirt. "He's told me about you." He did not offer up what sort of things he might have said, but the conclusions he had drawn were evident in his frown.

I maintained my easy smile. "You as well," I said. "I've heard a great deal about your work." The walls and shelves of his shop bore a profusion of taxidermies of creatures familiar and otherwise, their glassy eyes peering down at us. I saw an ibis posed in a bowing supplication, wings spread as if to curtsy, but something in the cock of its head suggested impishness.

"Giovanni!" Matteo bellowed, and his voice filled the whole of the musty space.

A head peeked out from the loft, tacking first to Matteo and then, perhaps slightly slower, to me. "I'll be down in a moment," my muse said.

While we waited, I amused myself with the thought of how repugnant the creature before me would be to drink. My tastes had become quite picky. Before I had left the Families, I had drank as we all had: nameless, faceless blood served in goblets, the source of which was never shown to us. I knew the Families had some system for it, some income stream of disposable bodies they could drain or some other such horror. It had never much troubled me then. The blood all tasted largely the same, nourishing and thick, but not unique beyond that. I had not given this any thought before I had begun feeding on my own, and only then did my eyes open to the wealth that was denied us.

The blood of any individual takes on the quality of their life. The correlations were indirect; other than strong-smelling foods like garlic and onions which were obviously anathema, the blood did not generally come to taste exactly like the food they consumed, but there was a correspondence in character between what someone puts in their body and what later flows through their veins. I had drunk from alcoholics whose blood made me stumble and slur my words, from heavy smokers and spat with the taste of pipe ash. I had enjoyed the unparalleled sweetness of healthy youth and the richer, full-bodied taste of age. There were as many flavors as there were people in the world, and when I discovered this, I vowed never to drink the lifeless stuff they fed us in the Families again.

This man before me absolutely stank of onion. It takes a lot of the stuff to hurt one of my kind, but he positively reeked, and I suspected he'd leave me with indigestion.

He scowled at me as we waited in silence and I smiled warmly, appraising his work as if I could not taste his displeasure. Did he know what I was, or was he just protective, uncertain about his friend messing around with some noble? I thought the latter, though if it were the former I would have plunged my fangs into his throat without a second thought, onions or not.

"So," he said. "What do you do?"

Ah, so it was a class thing.

I turned to him. "I write, mostly. Spells and such. I'm also something of a scholar."

"Something of a scholar." If he was displeased by this, it was difficult to say. Well, no surprise that he would be bitter. Though plenty of us did work, most dabbled for fun in various pursuits rather than having any reason to fully apply ourselves.

"He recognized that Xavro's was in Hvarian," came Giovanni's voice, accompanied by the drumming of soles on wooden stairs. My muse unfolded himself from the loft and put one hand on the ceiling as he descended, careful not to disturb any of the bundles of drying herbs hanging there.

"Thank you for coming, Dorian." He stood before me and shook my hand while Matteo looked on. "Let me gather my things," he said, shuffling off and stuffing books and papers into a leather satchel.

"Where are you going?" asked Matteo.

"I believe Giovanni wanted to show me some things in the University's collection. Then I suspect we will have time for some dinner in gastown."

"Don't wait up for me, Matteo," said Giovanni, giving his friend a look. The mustachioed man crossed his muscular, hairy arms, face impassive. "Sorry," he said, turning to me. "Matteo can be a bit of a *chezze* sometimes." I didn't know what that meant, but from the way Matteo's face flushed ruddy-red, it had hit home.

Giovanni laughed. "Let's be off."

I rather glowed, walking beside him in the snow-strewn streets of the new year. His face flushed as well. Though I could not tell if it had anything to do with my presence or simply the cold, whipping wind, the sight of the blood suffusing his cheeks distracted me.

"Thank you for calling on me," I said. "I'm curious about what you have to show me."

"You called yourself a scholar," he said. "A student of history. We certainly have artifacts at the University to interest near anyone, and there are a few I'd be pleased to show you, but perhaps you can tell me more about what it is that you study."

My fingers twitched, thinking about the feel of his pulse under the pads of my fingertips. I stuffed them in my pockets.

"Certainly," I said, my mind racing for a suitable answer. In truth, my studies were largely related to my own kind, and especially the old days that the Families were so determined to suppress. My interest in them came from a combination of pride and prurience particular to my kin. I thought there was romance in the old tales of villages cowed by the fear of a single vampire, and the legends of vampire hunters whose named echoed even in our histories. The organization and rigor of the Families had none of the thrill of those old tales.

"Vampires," I told him, before I'd decided if it was a good idea. "I'm fascinated by the old tales. The world seems a much safer place nowadays, and yet..." I smiled. "I feel like something has been lost since the world spoken of in the past. Vampires have been my primary fascination for some time, but any of the old, mythological creatures are of great interest to me." I picked up steam as I allowed myself to be honest, a nervous energy vibrating along the lengths of my arms. "How much of what is written is myth and how much is truth?"

He looked at me with raised eyebrows, but then nodded. "There is much discrepancy between the world that was and the world that appears to be. Certainly you are not the only historian who wonders if the discrepancy lies with the histories themselves, or if the world could truly have changed so much in such a short time."

The winter morning drew towards afternoon, the sun slanting low in the sky and blinding me when I glanced towards him. I wished for cloud cover. Sunlight would not destroy me unless it were the height of summer and I were to stand outside without shelter for a prolonged time, but I did not appreciate the feeling on my face. I straightened my collar to protect my neck.

The city of Neunhausen rested silently around us, perhaps because it was only sixth-night. Most businesses were shut with cheery holiday proclamations, but the air smelled of the hearth-fires and spices of humans in the apartments above the shuttered storefronts. A great glut of food awaited me in those homes if only I could charm my way into them, and no one would suspect anything for another three or four nights, most likely. During the solstice and the ten nights after, deaths could go unnoticed for days or even weeks.

"I study change myself," he said, and my mind reluctantly returned from the prospect of a feast. I was hungry, I must admit.

109

Famished. I had been saving my appetite for Giovanni; I found that a hearty meal always tasted best on an empty stomach.

"There have been sea changes in language over the past era, a strange amount of them. Much of it can be attributed to the major geopolitical shifts, but also more subtle shifts in people and populace such as the slow but substantial migration of Tsullish from the shore inwards as the forest traveled inland and the larger and more diverse populations of cities like Neunhausen and Nepte, especially in terms of the swelling numbers of immigrants from Poq and the Northern Isle nations."

"So, a map of language migration?"

He shook his head. "That's part of it, but that's the mundane stuff. People have been mapping and tracking that for centuries, and while it's interesting to see how languages move and shift and travel with their users, that does not account for the shifts we have seen.

"This is a manner of shifting of ALL languages." His hands fluttered about the clasp of his satchel, pulling the flap back and looking through the papers inside while redirecting his gaze at the icy ground every few seconds. "I have an illustration—"

I put my gloved hand on his, trying to ignore the thirst that rose within me at the contact, even through the leather of my gloves. "Let's wait until we're inside somewhere warm, maybe with coffee, so you don't slip and crack your skull on the ice?"

...

I've become jaded in my many centuries of life.

There are few things that can stir the heart of the undead, not because we are heartless monsters, but simply because we have been around so long. The cocky cynicism of vampires in tales is truthful, but all the teachings of the church that attribute this to the vanity of the Devil are nonsense.

But this library, it impressed me. It rivaled even the libraries of the Families.

The bars of winter sunlight that came through the high windows gilded the spines of countless leather-bound books in cream and gold. No central beams held up the structure, which I found remarkable in the absence of arches and any other visible masonry to support the ceiling, painted with eye-catching illustrations of myths and legends, especially those pertaining to Neunhausen. I recognized the stern face of Mariah leading the Sisters of Penance across the icy gray waters of the Berge, the Tinner with her silvery mask and stiletto and a wild grin, and Carsius Pheron with their steam-engine.

The shelves stretched near to the ceiling, easily thirty feet tall and full to the very top with books. We entered the library from a landing nearly level with the tops of the shelves, which were, curiously, home to a forest of vines.

"The plants?" I asked.

"Scrivener's leaf," he said. "We can make ink from the sap."

"Don't they carry a risk of rot? That much dampness so close to books?"

He smiled. "You underestimate our engineers. Besides, these are curious plants; they tend to absorb moisture from the air, improving the conditions for our more delicate volumes."

"Scrivener's leaf indeed."

We stood there in silence for a few moments while a collection of silver-robed Scholars of Iron passed behind us, speaking in hushed, almost reverent voices.

Then he turned to me. "I have something to show you. Come with me."

He handed me the stake, and I very nearly dropped it.

Though it would need to be pounded through my chest to end my existence, there was power in it, and I feared to have it so near. It felt like it might leap into my chest of its own accord, such was the strength of its affinity.

It was poplar, he said, though I barely heard him. It stunk of ichor, and the smell of one of my kin's blood spilled set my own system into internal emergency. It took more willpower than I had realized I possessed to stand there, smiling, trying to look the appropriate amount interested rather than terrified for my very existence.

I took a deep breath, inhaling deeply of the bouquet of my muse, shaving soap, pine tar, and ink today. This made me a bit dizzier, but it steadied me in the present. My hands stopped shaking so severely and I was no longer at risk of dropping the stake. I was thankful that we were alone in his office; I had begun to fear the presence of his colleagues most interested in studying vampires and wondering if they would recognize me for what I was.

"Fascinating," I breathed."

"Are you all right?"

"Yes," I said. "It can just be... overwhelming to see an artifact in real life."

"You said the Barrowlord was a great source of interest to you."

"Yes." And in this, I told the truth. He had been a hunter in another era, a hero to humans, but a nightmare to my kind. In some ways, he was the quintessential legend of a hunter, tripping demons up with the clever wording of his bonds to them, seducing vampires, and destroying them. "Perhaps it's a bit stereotypical for a student of these things, but I find the legends all too irresistible."

He nodded. "My colleague Yvette studies the historicity of his legends. She is fascinated by the truth behind the myth."

"Oh yes? And what has she found?"

"That, like with many legends, they seem to persist even in the absence of all forms of physical evidence for or against. Which is to say, not much, I'm afraid. But perhaps that is good; I admit that it would be quite disappointing to discover that he had, say, only killed a few vampires in quite standard ways rather than the countless foes he tackled through all his many stories." He tapped the stake. "Yvette claims that they have found the ichor of almost fifteen different individual vampires on this stake."

"Not one for waste, our Barrowlord," I said. I looked up at Giovanni, at his dark eyes, heavy with bags, his wry grin. I thought that he could easily bring about my own death, were he inclined to try. I had the startling realization that Giovanni himself could be a hunter, one who took me for what I was and had constructed an elaborate game to get close to me. The paranoia tried to rise in me, but something else tamped it down, some slower, easier feeling that flowed when I met his eyes.

Perhaps it would be all right, I thought, if he was. I wondered at those words I had burned in my stove, not for the first time, but they existed only as sleep-shadows. I could not even be certain I had woken up and written and that it had not simply been a dream.

He glanced out the window to where the sunset was just beginning to make itself known in the west, tinting the afternoon with light golds and oranges. "We've been at this for a while," he said, "and work makes me thirsty. How about we go find something to drink? Maybe something to eat?"

I handed him back the stake, perhaps quicker than I had intended, and I thought I saw a flash of something in his eyes, but then it was gone. "Yes," I said. "Let's, please."

He slid his finger over the mirror, gathering up the spare crumbs of cocaine that we had missed, and rubbed it on his gums with a detachment that I found intoxicating.

"What's this?" I murmured, my fingers brushing the shiny, darker brown of scar on his narrow hip. His breathing, the way his chest fluttered against mine as I ran my fingers below his waistband, was nearly enough to drive me wild.

"Tried to steal from a cathedral, when I was a student," he said, voice husky. "You know. Lots of gold. Candlesticks are usually the easiest. Got the watchman's schedule wrong. He came through the nave five minutes too early." His eyes met mine, narrow, playful. "I got a knife for my trouble."

"You're lucky that's all you got."

He smiled devilishly and squirmed away from me, leaning back towards the neat white lines I had cut. The cocaine did nothing for me, but I faked it and let him have most of it. His vice had been obvious from the first, and it hadn't taken much to procure him some, there in that tiny upper room from the drinking hole we'd found ourselves in the depths of the night.

I pulled my shirt off, and I watched the way his shining eyes drank me in greedily. His desire for me was obvious, as, certainly, was mine for him, and I danced on the edge of the madness of bloodlust, running my fingertips along his skin and making him shiver.

He sniffed hard and leaned back onto the bed, a look of bliss on his face. His eyes were fiery, lit with some preternatural light, and I thought I saw a challenge in them.

So be it. I smiled dangerously wide and leaned over to swallow him whole.

Before an audience, reading. All those wide eyes, lost, letting me lead them without thought. I had never found it necessary to imbibe alcohol, for the intoxication that came with such command of others was more draught than I could handle, at times.

I found myself in a caesura, a brief cresting of the wave of the present that returned my ego to me for a glimpse of the room in which I read. Lady Kauhane had kept Heart's-End in its traditional furnishings, a style at once simple and elegant: braided hempen rope banded in gold, furniture of light rattan with inlays of mother-of-pearl and silver, her servants in light linen goru and tied silken sashes, ears and noses pierced with jewels of jade and iridescent wing casings from pepper-beetles.

The Lady herself sat near the front, her husband's small, shapely hand cradled between her own, laughter in the apples of her cheeks and rapture in her eyes. Much of the audience was her family, as I read for the health of her cousin's newborns on their naming-day, but other nobles sat among the countless honey-brown cheeks and falls of straight, gleaming, dark hair.

Lady Alynse sat between two of her handmaidens, though rumor persisted that their closeness belied more than a simple relationship of mistress and serving-women. From the way the two younger women inclined their bodies towards her and how the Lady herself seemed to expand to fill the space that separated them, such rumors could be true.

Lord Coilsbury and his wife, the famous engineer, Sadae, sat with eyes fixed on me but some tension pulling them apart. They sat together, but in the way one sits next to a stranger on a bench, with every intention of not touching.

Lord Forsythe sat near the very front as well, for which I was not surprised, and he wore a look of open awe.

Many wondered whether I courted Lord Forsythe, him being young and eligible and a patron of the arts. It was one of many rumors that surrounded me; my appearance in the courts of Neunhausen had been a sudden thing and unheralded by any known lineage or any duchy changing hands.

Though you might think such a high profile social standing a strange way to hide, I found it superior to the anonymity I might have achieved in the working classes. Courtly types are gossips, but they adore mystery and I endeavored to make myself as mysterious as I could. This was in many ways simpler than the alternative, as well. No records existed of me in the archives of any noble family's lineage. No travel receipts, nothing in the news beyond the present. I had considered planting the needed evidence to show my ascent from some lower social strata, perhaps a changed name somewhere or photographs of myself on some tenant farm, but in time I came to realize that the mystery was a stronger shield than the evidence would be. Though there were certainly those nobles who delighted in unearthing the proof of a previous life before the courts and dangling it before a newly made Lord, the desire for mystery would keep them from looking too hard.

And regardless, I have a taste for luxury.

Lord Forsythe was much to my tastes as well: a polymath with a focus on philosophy and a fondness for spoken-word poetry and theater. The red and black velvet of his tailcoat, his light brown skin, gray-green eyes, and teasing grin. His broodwife had borne for him one heir already, a beautiful copper-haired child and was pregnant with a second, but their relationship was one of comfort and not of romance. He had a mind at once brilliant and elegant, and I often thought that, were I a mortal, he might be well-matched to me.

It was a shame. He would have made great sport as prey, as his cleverness would have kept him ahead of my machinations for some time. But I had made a rule to never hunt nobility with whom I associated publicly.

I watched the way his eyes widened and a self-satisfied smile crossed his lips, hearing my words. He assumed, as they all did, that my poetry was for him.

Let him assume, I thought. The memory of Giovanni's surprise as I pressed my card into his palm, and the heady smell of the warmth of him, and the blood that flowed beneath his skin that I ached to spill, crossed my mind. I smiled warmly and bowed as applause showered me like a warm summer rain.

Lady Kauhane approached me after the reading, her long, black hair gathered and bound in a shining net of sapphires, bearing a crystal tumbler in her gray silk gloved hands.

"I was just speaking to Lord Wexford about you. She tells me you are particular to Scotch," she said with a smile, handing me the glass. "Your words have cast a spell over the night."

I nodded, wondering if she knew the deeper truth of those words as they left her tongue. "You are too kind, my lady."

"She has much to say about your work," Lady Kauhane continued, looping an arm through mine and threading me through the sobered crowd. The eyes that met mine glanced down, meek, now. "And I must say that while I believed her, it was not until now that I understood." Her eyes were dark, too, and they set my mind to wondering about a certain someone else, and wondering what he might be doing as I strolled with the Lady of Heart's-End.

She led me through the French doors and out to the swept flagstones to the south of the house. The night was cold, the stars scattered like dust in rich navy heavens.

She looked around, at the dark gray stone of Heart's-End, at the fields swept with a smoothness of fresh snow. "It must be a comfort," she said.

I fought the urge to laugh at the idea that anything about that night might be a comfort to me. "My Lady?" I asked.

"To know something will live on beyond you," she said. "We will all die, some of us sooner than others. But you will live on in your words." She shrugged her stole around her shoulders, the warm light from the house catching in the rich fur as it shifted on her well-muscled shoulders.

"Certainly you will live on too, in name and in the bones of Heart's-End," I said.

She laughed, a tinkling, bitter sound, far from the booming richness I had heard earlier in the night.

"My name will live on, I suppose. Lady Kekepania Kauhane, seventeenth Lady of the House of Kauhane and Mistress of Heart's-End. Hah." Her smile looked like I felt, something soured. "And what truth of me exists in that? I will join my mother and grandmother, names writ in the stones of this place. But a name, a title, that is the least measure of us, wouldn't you say?"

I said nothing to this. I suppressed the thing that wanted to burble out of me, uncertain if it was laughter or tears.

"Your words capture your essence in a way a name simply cannot. A name is something given to you before you can even speak, before you exist as anything more than squalling potential. Perhaps in your lifetime, those around you will come to associate your name with who you are, and for a chosen few, your name will live on in the public consciousness, attached to your deeds and bearing with it some virtues or vices, though even then, future generations will see you through a lens that distorts you into stories and myths.

"But your writing, your words will be read by those in the future. And even if your name were not attached, even if your words survived only in anonymous scraps forgotten in the bowels of a library, someone reading them would have the measure of your soul." Her searching eyes pressed on my soul, and I turned to meet them. "Certainly, this must bring you comfort."

She asked for herself more than for me, so I nodded. "It does, indeed."

How could I explain that the idea of my words enduring me filled me with a sense of despair for the future?

She did not know that the idea kept me awake into the black well of morning, that I burned my notebooks, fearful for anyone to read the truth within them. I never used the Gift to pull an unwilling victim into subservience. I always found the idea of such blatant manipulation artless and dull. But I used it often to tilt things in my favor. My words were indeed the measure of me as a man.

I smiled at her, hoping to show that I had been complimented by her words, and I decided it was time to depart.

"My Lady," I said, "I prefer to maintain an air of mystery, and I'm certain Lord Forsythe will seek my attention after my reading. I'd like to make a discrete exit." My words sounded fake to my ears, a pathetic excuse, but her face lit up.

"Certainly, certainly," she said, ushering me before her and down the stairs onto the grass. "Do you have a carriage awaiting you?"

"No," I said. Which was true. I had other, subtler means of transport.

"You might hail one down in the town. It's no more than a mile on foot. There are old hunting trails in the woods that the children use for their games. Follow the line of lilacs down to the gate by the trees. The woods are dark, but the full moon should provide you light. Would you like a torch?"

I shook my head. Night stretched before me, clear as day, and while it made more sense to take a torch to maintain my appearance as human, I thought it would only add to the legend. "Thank you, my Lady."

"Think nothing of it," she said with a grin. "Off with you, now. I'll go capture his attention so that he doesn't come looking until you're long since gone." She tipped me a wink, and I made my way into the comfortable night.

There came, then, some weeks, some months perhaps, that I would prefer to summarize without detail. Let me say only that Giovanni and I saw one another many times, often intimately, always sharing the depths of our passions and our knowledge. Many evenings spent in his office, him teaching me about his studies, leading to tenderness by the hearth. Winter gave way to the first pale blushings of spring.

I did not drink of him. I did not reveal my true nature. Perhaps you already see the fool I had become. I had come to believe, perhaps, that there was an option that did not lead to his destruction or mine. I drank of others in that time out of need, but the hunts were dull and without interest to me compared to the time I spent with Giovanni.

In short, I had fallen in love. More fool, me.

The velvet dark of evening unrolled before us, looking out from the high, cold glass of the parlor windows. Few words had passed between us since we had arrived, his eyes widening when the manor house came into view through the carriage window and then looking at me, narrowed. The brief tour, showing him where he might ring a servant, use the privy, set his belongings, was conducted largely in silence, and now we stood in my study with a fire burning in the hearth as the early spring night drew in close around us.

He had not been to my manor before. With other prey, I had often brought them by quickly, to awe them and leave them off balance and desiring my attention and favor, but with Giovanni, those tactics seemed churlish and overwrought. I was no longer drawn to the same amusements as I had once been.

"So," he said, turning from the window to me, where I sat in a wingback chair pretending to read.

I looked up at him, raising an eyebrow, saying nothing.

"There's something you haven't told me," he said.

I wondered how much he knew, but I thought it might be time for honesty. "There is."

"Then let's have it."

"Very well." I closed my book, looked at him. "My interest in vampires—"

"You are one of them," he said, cutting me off.

What could I say to that? I nodded.

He scoffed, crossing his arms. "You've planned this well, then," he said, his voice dull, his arms angular with tension. "I suppose this is where you will... what? Drain me empty? Kill me? Imprison me to keep me for food?" He pulled off his spectacles and rubbed his other hand across his face with a look of weariness.

"How long have you known?"

"Since the day in my office when you nearly dropped the stake. You claimed it was awe, but the fear was written plain on your face." He sighed, standing and pacing. "I had suspicions from the start, you know. You're deathly pale and far too handsome to have taken a true interest in me. I thought at first you might be a charlatan or confidence man, but over time, as no money-grabbing scheme materialized, I began to worry it was something else." He took off his glasses and rubbed his face. "I can't believe I came with you."

"I can't believe you did, either, if you knew." I shut the book and placed it to the side of me. "Why did you?"

He shook his head. "I suppose I didn't know until we arrived."

"What gave it away?"

"The kitchens," he said. "They are pristine. The pots and pans are stacked so neatly. The counters are spotless."

"Could we not keep a tidy kitchen?"

"It's not the tidiness so much as it is the emptiness. There's a lived-in quality to a kitchen, an arranging of things for efficiency. Your kitchen looks like a picture of a kitchen."

"They are using the kitchen now," I said. "Dinner should be ready within the hour."

"Well, take a look for yourself when they're done. See what's left where. It won't look the same." He sighed, looking around at the high ceiling of the parlor. "This is a beautiful place," he said. "I suppose that gave it away, too. You've no duchy to your name, and yet you have a manor house befitting a landed lord. How, might I ask, did you acquire this place?"

I smiled sadly. "Your first guess would likely be correct."

And now, how could I explain I had hoped to woo him with this place? Perhaps my means of acquiring it involved the untimely death of the previous owner, but I had not killed out of meaninglessness. "The Lord who owned this place was a boor," I said. "This house is seven centuries old. It dates from the late Revitalization period."

"The stonework is exquisite," he said. "Too costly to do that kind of construction today, and yet I suspect even a house this large is quite easy to heat. I should like to inspect it more closely." He gave me a sour smile. "Assuming I had the time."

"The previous owner had no respect for this glorious place," I said. "He'd inherited it from his father, being his only heir. It was quite a sad story; the son was a wastrel, gone off to the Eastern colonies in the name of adventure. He was fond of drinking and carousing and had no respect for the arts or for history."

Giovanni sat on the divan opposite me, leaning forward, clasping his hands over his knees. Despite the new tension I saw banding his shoulders, his eyes sparked with interest. Guilt churned within me, the realization that this was still so easy, even when he understood.

"His father had Craster's."

"No second child for him, then," said Giovanni.

"Just so." I sipped my glass of port.

"So you were doing him a favor."

"I wondered if the son might've considered his hell-raising his own legacy," I said. "He seemed poised to tear this place down, no mean feat given its construction. He'd already done a great deal of damage to the northernmost wing by the time I arrived, though thankfully nothing permanent. I am given to believe he had been looking for spellcrofters and had come upon none who would parley with him, once they understood the nature of what he was asking." I smiled. "That detail does bring lightness into my heart."

"Heart." Giovanni's smile twisted.

I continued, as if the word hadn't wounded me. "It was under this guise I entered. It was easy, really. Though I doubt the Gift would ever allow me to write the destruction of this place, it was not hard to demonstrate my talents to him." I wove my fingers together. "It was over within the evening."

"And you came to inherit this place?" His expression was a sneering disbelief.

"I allowed the Gift to determine what would happen. Apparently, it decided I was a reasonable benefactor and teased the lineages and documents enough to grant me evidence of my inheritance. All closed documents, of course, but I am the lawful owner."

Giovanni was silent. A servant appeared to tend the fire.

"Would you like something to drink?" I ventured. "The cellars are well-stocked."

"Something tawny," he said. The servant nodded, feeding the hearth, and then disappeared through a door.

Silence stretched between us again, and Giovanni relaxed back on the couch, looking at the fire. In time, he spoke again. "I suppose your family name isn't really Allwether, is it?"

I smiled. "I was born Dorian Highfallow," I said. It would not take a historian to recognize a Family name. He nodded, not looking away from the fire. The servant brought his drink, and he accepted it without speaking.

"Dinner will be ready in a moment, sir," he said to me.

"Shall we?" I asked Giovanni.

Giovanni sipped his port and then turned to me slowly. "History remembers what the Families would have us all forget," he said. He unfolded himself from the couch and stood. I followed suit, buttoning my coat. "The records of who you are... What you are... They are purged from all but the most ancient of sources. There is a gap, make no mistake. Unexplained deaths. Bounties and jobs to hunt monsters of which there is no other record. Preventative measures to take against your kind. But so little detail as to who you are. A casual reader could easily write these things off as the inanities of the premodern mind, but those of us who seek to reconstruct the past see what has been removed and we know the shape of it."

"All the power and influence in the world cannot change the past. It may only change our record of it."

He nodded. "Let's eat, then," he said, and he took my arm.

"You are so cold," he whispered, and I ran my fingertips along the goosebumps that raised on his bare back.

"Such is my nature," I murmured against his neck.

"Is this it, then?" he whispered, his head pulled back taut, eyes staring at the ceiling.

I brushed my lips along his throat, smelling the sweet warmth of the healthy arteries, imagining their gentle give as I might sink my fangs in, the small knife nearby in case my filed canines were not up to the task. I kissed the skin gently. "This is it," I said softly. "But it need not be the end."

I felt him tense at this. "You are forbidden," he said.

"Members of the Families are forbidden," I said. "But I have been long since excommunicated."

"I somehow doubt this makes it square with them," he said.

"Certainly not." I allowed my fingertips to trace the length of his naked body, lit orange and shaded deep blue from the glowing hearth. "If I were not already thought destroyed, this would mark me ten times over." I ran my tongue along the groove in his throat where I knew the blood ran most thickly. "You as well." He shuddered beneath me. "But you would not be alone. We would be together. There are ways we might hide. I am quite adept at it, now. You would be in danger, but no more danger than I."

"Every time you feed, you put yourself in more danger," he said.

"There are less dangerous ways to feed," I said. "I do what I do for sport and for the poetry of it. But it is dangerous, and one does tire." And how could I explain that he had changed something in me? That my desire to dominate him, to watch the shininess leave his eyes when he was drained dry, had evaporated? That perhaps I sought something that I had so long mocked: stability, comfort, and the company of a mind that brought me joy.

"There are places we might go," I said. "There are philters that allow our kind to feed on ram's blood. On boar's blood. It is not as luxurious, but it is safer."

"Our kind," he said. "As if you've chosen for me."

A beat, another caesura. Threads of story in my mind, red with blood. I wondered in vain about the words I had burned, if they spoke of this moment. I wondered if any fault could be said to lie with me.

"I will not choose for you," I said.

A beat of silence.

"I say no, what becomes of me?"

I had planned, of course, to drain him, but my lips against his hot flesh betrayed me. "The stablemaster will arrange a carriage to take you wherever you want to go," I said, and I told the truth. "I will not follow you or contact you again."

He said nothing to this, but caught my lips in a kiss.

A rhythm building in intensity, then, and banishing the chill of night. Banishing the chill of my own cursed form, and bringing warmth, even briefly.

I woke before dawn to find him gone.

FAREWELL

ABOUT THE AUTHOR

Simon Shadows is a queer and trans author, illustrator, and demon prince living in the gloomy gray of Portland, Oregon. Outside of alchemizing his dreams and visions into strange art and fiction, he loves watching anime, listening to filthy metal, and learning to identify all the plants and animals he possibly can.

Sign up for his free email list
WHISPERS FROM THE SHADOWS
to keep up with new book releases, behind-the-scenes info, blog posts, and more!

→ **https://www.simonshado.ws** ←

Made in the USA
Monee, IL
25 April 2023

32449159R00085